"You don't thi~~~~~~~~ benefits for your sister in the arrangement?"

"None that are worth it."

Elodie had long ago vowed never to get involved with another man again. She'd fought hard for her own freedom. She'd done horrible, necessary things. But she would suffer far more if it could save her sister from the same.

"For some unfathomable reason you want to get married," she said. "So perhaps it doesn't matter who the unfortunate woman is."

He was unnervingly still, that intensity sharpening his eyes. "You have another candidate in mind?"

Candidate. As if it were a job. "Another poor soul, you mean?"

The devastating good looks of the man, his searing wealth, his callous lack of care and her own horrendously *animal* response to him fueled her fury to the point where all control was lost.

"Sure," she added acidly. "If you want a wife so *desperately*, then you can marry me!"

A brand-new and exciting trilogy from USA TODAY
bestselling author Natalie Anderson.

Convenient Wives Club

Once bitten... Twice a bride!

Disastrous first marriages taught friends Elodie,
Phoebe and Bethan one important lesson. From
now on, the only commitment they'll be making is
to each other and their friendship. And the only vow
they'll be making is *never* to say "I do" again—for as
long as they shall live.

But all three women will be made to break their
promise...

Realizing her parents are forcing her little sister into
a convenient marriage, Elodie is determined not to
let her sibling suffer the same fate she once had.
Her solution? Offering herself to the groom as the
bride. The problem? She's got the wrong man!

Their Altar Arrangement
Available now!

And look out for Phoebe's and Bethan's stories,
coming soon!

THEIR ALTAR
ARRANGEMENT

NATALIE ANDERSON

Harlequin

PRESENTS

If you purchased this book without a cover you should be aware that this book is stolen property. It was reported as "unsold and destroyed" to the publisher, and neither the author nor the publisher has received any payment for this "stripped book."

Harlequin® PRESENTS™

ISBN-13: 978-1-335-63152-7

Their Altar Arrangement

Recycling programs for this product may not exist in your area.

Copyright © 2025 by Natalie Anderson

All rights reserved. No part of this book may be used or reproduced in any manner whatsoever without written permission.

Without limiting the author's and publisher's exclusive rights, any unauthorized use of this publication to train generative artificial intelligence (AI) technologies is expressly prohibited.

This is a work of fiction. Names, characters, places and incidents are either the product of the author's imagination or are used fictitiously. Any resemblance to actual persons, living or dead, businesses, companies, events or locales is entirely coincidental.

For questions and comments about the quality of this book, please contact us at CustomerService@Harlequin.com.

TM and ® are trademarks of Harlequin Enterprises ULC.

Harlequin Enterprises ULC
22 Adelaide St. West, 41st Floor
Toronto, Ontario M5H 4E3, Canada
www.Harlequin.com

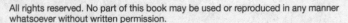

Printed in U.S.A.

USA TODAY bestselling author **Natalie Anderson** writes emotional contemporary romance full of sparkling banter, sizzling heat and uplifting endings—perfect for readers who love to escape with empowered heroines and arrogant alphas who are too sexy for their own good. When she's not writing, you'll find Natalie wrangling her four children, three cats, two goldfish and one dog... and snuggled in a heap on the sofa with her husband at the end of the day. Follow her at natalie-anderson.com.

Books by Natalie Anderson

Harlequin Presents

The Night the King Claimed Her
The Boss's Stolen Bride
My One-Night Heir

Jet-Set Billionaires

Revealing Her Nine-Month Secret

Billion-Dollar Christmas Confessions

Carrying Her Boss's Christmas Baby

Innocent Royal Runaways

Impossible Heir for the King
Back to Claim His Crown

Billion-Dollar Bet

Billion-Dollar Dating Game

Visit the Author Profile page
at Harlequin.com for more titles.

For the two Sorayas,

Soraya L—our daily accountability texts are the bomb.

Soraya B—your guidance is just the best.

Thank you both so very much!!!

CHAPTER ONE

ELODIE WALLACE STOOD in the heart of London. A stretch of ludicrously expensive stone residences curved before her, the city homes of many of the world's wealthiest, those supposedly important, probably corrupt, definitely powerful people. The kind of autocrats who'd do anything to ensure their wealth and power didn't just remain intact for all eternity but grew like rampant weeds through millennia—strangling anything and anyone in the way of their relentlessly upward trajectories.

Cynical? Why yes, Elodie was. Dramatic? That too.

But sometimes in life everything does happen all at once. Bad things truly happened 'in threes', and 'when it rains, it pours' wasn't a strong enough forecast—a whole hurricane had hit her world. It wasn't enough that her dream career was under threat or that her best friend's livelihood was also at risk, but her younger's sister's *life* was basically at stake.

So she would enter the den. Slay the dragon.

Save the princess. Though admittedly now she was confronted by the imposing buildings that so spectacularly signposted both wealth and sticking power, she regretted not bringing backup. But both Phoebe and Bethan, her *compadres* in pursuing a life of personal liberty, needed protecting too. Phoebe was away taking the first holiday in her life, while Bethan was still fragile from a deeply wounding disillusionment. So Elodie had not told them about the call she'd taken from her sister Ashleigh late last night, nor of the decision she'd made to come here today.

One step at a time.

The clichés would get her through, they usually did. She loved using them at work—twisting them to mean the opposite and thus confusing her customers. She stalked along the pristine path until she hit the right numeral beautifully painted in black on twin marble columns. The portico was ridiculously grand, the neoclassical architectural style exuding timeless and impenetrable exclusivity.

She registered the security cameras. They were subtly situated but still able to be seen, thus acting as deterrent as much as actual recording devices. Breaching this citadel would be a challenge. She drew breath and climbed, staring straight into the lens of the camera nearest the front door as she pressed the button.

Somewhat amazingly the door opened after

only a few moments. Elodie's attention zipped to the man blocking the space. He looked like a cross between a pro wrestler and a secret service agent. Blank expression, black earpiece, built physique complete with a bulky bit in his black jacket that made her suspect he was carrying a weapon. That last might be her over-active imagination but she was pretty sure. Quelling her rising nerves, she fixed her gaze squarely on him. She'd pretend she was meant to be there, as if *she* were someone important too. She was good at pretending.

'Elodie Wallace,' she announced with the particularly precise enunciation she used at work. 'I'm here to see Ramon Fernandez.'

'Snootily confident attitude' crossed with 'bulletproof ballbreaker facade' had got her into some of the most exclusive clubs when she'd needed to destroy her own name. But, bold as she'd been on those nights, she had to be even more so now.

'Is he expecting you?' More than a touch of scepticism tarnished the man's reply.

'I'm his fiancée's sister,' Elodie elaborated crisply. 'I'm here to discuss the arrangements for this weekend's engagement party.'

The butler/bodybuilder/probable assassin might've been immaculately trained but even he failed to hide his startled moment at her answer. Elodie maintained her frigidly polite expression. Bluffing was an art form and fortunately she'd had plenty of practice. There was a pause. Though he kept his gaze on her, the man's eye muscles narrowed slightly and she sensed his attention was elsewhere. His earpiece perhaps? She tilted her chin slightly. She wasn't leaving without talking to the man she was sure was inside. She'd chain herself to one of these columns and scream like a banshee if required. Ashleigh's future literally hung in the balance.

The behemoth drew an audible breath but suddenly muttered, 'Of course.'

Was he talking to her or—?

He stepped back. 'Please come in.'

As she followed him inside she sneaked another steadying breath, unable to appreciate the sudden temperature change from the stifling summer heat outside to a cool, high-ceilinged sanctuary of an atrium.

The body-built butler gestured towards a comfortable-looking chair. 'Please take a seat.'

'I'd prefer to stand.' She smiled glacially. 'While you let him know I'm here.'

'He knows you're here.'

A prickle of fear scored its way down Elodie's spine. Had he been watching the feed from those cameras? The butler paused again, this time not even trying to hide that he was listening to someone. Elodie stood defiantly but her already erratic pulse zipped from rapid to frantic. Cold sweat slicked across her skin.

'If you'll follow me,' the man said, abandoning any attempt to hide his wide-eyed curiosity, 'Señor Fernandez is ready for you.'

She very much doubted that. Ramon Fernandez was the man Elodie's parents were bullying her baby sister into marrying and she intended to eviscerate him.

Although now she was actually *here* she realised she had little concrete idea as to *how*.

She followed the man, reluctantly impressed by the interior. She'd expected ostentatious decor—a gallery of gilt-edged frames housing priceless portraits, gleaming sculptures on plinths, luxurious rugs handmade by a city of workers a century ago…that sort of thing. But this home was sleek with black-painted walls and dark polished wooden floors, punctuated by occasional warm lights that only partially illuminated the way. It made Elodie feel as if the world were growing gloomier with every step—as if she were being led into a lair. A dark, sumptuous dwelling for a predator.

Way too fanciful… Elodie mocked herself.

This wasn't one of the escape rooms she designed and managed. Though she memorised the way as she went in case she needed to actually escape in a hurry. She tugged her blazer sleeves and swept her hands down her tailored pants. The sleek suit formed part of her armour as did the make-up she'd applied only half an hour ago. She'd had to mask the shadowy ravages of an utterly sleepless night. The bustier beneath her blazer was extremely well-fitting—literally giving strength to her spine. Black and embellished with orange and gold beads and yes, while those did completely clash with her red hair, that was deliberate too. She wanted to project fearlessness. That she was a rule breaker. Reckless. A possible threat. Indeed, she wore it to project intimidation. But it was pure projection. A ploy because deception was her trade. But today wasn't mere playful pretence, she needed the armour for real and it was burnished with rage.

'Señor Fernandez...' The butler paused just outside a wide open doorway. 'Ms Wallace is here to see you.'

'How delightful.'

A drawl. Complete mockery.

Elodie froze on the threshold, barely aware of the butler's departure behind her as the man stood up from the sleek desk that housed a bank of slimline screens.

Blue eyes. Black hair. The sharpest cheekbones she'd ever seen. Not chiselled but sliced—angular, masculine, stunning. Eagle-eyed, he stared back at her. For a timeless moment she just stared back. Then he moved. She didn't. Couldn't.

For a split second she felt a hit of *hope*. Surely this man couldn't be the monster her sister meant? Ashleigh had described him as slimy and weak. Elodie had gone online to track down his London address but there had been little else and so nothing had prepared her for the cinematic perfection of Ramon Fernandez. He looked like Hollywood's version of the ultimate, suave hero.

She blinked. It didn't help. The tuxedo amped up his attractiveness. Formal evening wear suited most men—maximised their height, breadth, length—but this suit did all that and more for him. His frame was leaner than the butler's but she suspected his muscles were no less lethal and he had an air of command the other man lacked. But it was those eyes and the aquiline features that mesmerised her.

'You're *far* too old for her,' she breathed, so stunned that her first thought simply fell out of her mouth in a puff of disbelief.

Not just too old. Too *everything*. Too wealthy. Too handsome. Too successful, surely. Because he was smug with it. She watched him stroll towards her, his demeanour relaxed yet predatory, as he calmly took in every aspect of *her* appearance. He enjoyed wielding his power and he had it in spades. Both personal and professional. *Why* on earth would a man who lived in a place like this and looked like he did, need to buy himself a teenage bride?

'Do you think?' he asked conversationally.

So it was true. He didn't even try to deny the arrangement. Bitter disappointment squashed that little leap of hope and her rage returned. But still she couldn't move.

Undeniably overwhelming, he was tall, dark, intolerably, impossibly handsome.

Yes, a cliché. But again, the cliché was flipped. Like the conundrums she created, Elodie's exterior ran at a complete counterpoint to her interior. While she projected a confident demeanour, on the inside she was terrified. This man was the same but in a far worse reverse. Beneath the beauty, this man was a beast. Angelic on the outside, a monster within. It was knowing this that caused her heart to stop altogether, right? The absolute horror before her. She almost lost her nerve.

'You realise she's only *just* turned eighteen,' she spat contemptuously.

He stopped less than a foot from her. Much closer and he'd be breaching generally accepted boundaries of polite personal space. Not that he apparently gave a damn given the arrogance oozing from him. Doubtless he considered himself not just above convention but above the law.

'You realise she only left school a few weeks ago?' she added when he still didn't bother to reply. 'She's beautiful, but she's a baby.'

His gaze dropped, lingering on the beadwork of her bustier. He was looking at her like he was assessing an item for the art collection he didn't even have. But his was a keen, knowing eye—summing up her valuation with a singular glance and to her shock and mortification a torrent of re-action released within her. She *blushed*—actually blushed. Heat rose everywhere as she endured his remorseless appraisal. Her response was fierce and uncontrolled—appalled outrage, right? Not any other kind of response.

'You have nothing to say to that?' she goaded desperately.

'I thought you wished to discuss the arrange-ments for the engagement party, not her age.' A cool reproof.

Her jaw dropped for a split second before her wild anger unleashed, driving her forward into the room so she stood toe to toe with the monster. 'There shouldn't *be* an engagement party! If you had *any* scruples you'd end this deal.'

He cocked his head ever so slightly and looked down his nose at her. 'Deal?'

It was that smallest curl of a smile that did it.

'I know all about it,' she derided furiously, any last self-restraint in flames. 'I know you're *pay-ing* for your bride.'

'You think?'

How could he be so sanguine?

The intensity of her anger overrode everything. 'You're investing in my parents' hotel. Which is madness. Surely you're aware it's never been a commercial success. Some would say it's a lemon. Why do you want it?'

He remained relaxed. 'Surely you know how good I am with hotels—'

'Right, I do. So forgive me if I don't believe that you need another one. Certainly not one that isn't anywhere near the size of those already in your stable.' She glared at him.

'Perhaps I like a challenge,' he said quietly.

'You're bored? You need entertaining?' she said sarcastically. 'Join a Scrabble club. Better yet, hire a children's party entertainer.'

Something flickered in his eyes, but she couldn't quite define it and he still said nothing.

'No?' she mocked. 'Because it's another sort of filly you want, isn't it?'

His beautiful lips curved again.

She shook her head in total disbelief. 'Why do you need a wife, exactly? Is it image management? Because in case you hadn't worked it out, I'm going to be a problem here.' The only thing she could think was to shame him. She knew too well that shame was a vitriolic thing. 'I'll go to the media,' she added. 'I'll cause such a scandal, I'll—'

'Publicly embarrass your own family?'

She stared into his intense blue gaze. Clearly he didn't know that she'd already embarrassed her family on a professional level. Entirely deliberately, knowing they'd disown her. Because four years ago this had happened to *her*. She hadn't been eighteen, but nineteen when her father had driven her into the arms of a man she didn't love. He'd always been controlling—from the subjects she studied at school, to the clothes she wore, to how she spent every moment of her time. He was the head of the family and Elodie, her sister and her mother were expected to do his bidding without question. Elodie had long accepted that as normal, but in her late teens her frustration grew. Her father had never valued her as anything more than a decorative source of free labour. He'd never listened to her ideas for the hotel. And *she'd* barely paid attention to Callum Henderson. Yes, he'd been at her school, but he was three years older and honestly off her radar. Not her father's though. Son of the local mayor, monied and influential. Her father had been thrilled to recruit him as assistant manager. Elodie had been hurt her father had laughed at her own quietly voiced inclination to apply.

But Callum had gone out of his way to talk to Elodie. He'd told her about a couple of interactions between them at school. Truthfully, she'd never even remembered them. He'd listened to her ideas—even enacted a couple—presenting them to her father as his purely to get them over the line. To Elodie's surprise her father hadn't been angry about Callum taking her time—he'd told her to be nice to him. For once she seemed to have pleased him.

The proposal had come out of the blue—a

rose-petal-strewn moment in front of her parents and half the hotel staff. Blindsided, there was no way she could reject Callum *publicly*. Especially not when she'd glimpsed the hard expectation in her father's eyes and realised that he hadn't just known about it but that he'd *approved* it. She'd had to say yes in the moment. And then her father wouldn't hear her misgivings. She would never 'do better' and Callum was going to invest in the much-needed hotel upgrade and she couldn't be the one to deny the rest of her family that much-needed resource; moreover, she should be *honoured* someone like him wanted someone like her.

At that point Callum hadn't even kissed her. It had never occurred to Elodie that he'd want to. But he'd been patient and persuasive. He'd promised to manage her father once they were married. And here's where Elodie had been so at fault herself. She'd been flattered because he'd listened, because he'd seemed to truly care. She'd believed him, blind to the fact that what he wanted wasn't what she really was. So swiftly she'd been swept into a situation she couldn't escape.

The gravity of her mistake hit within mere days of the marriage. Callum's promised support and freedom had been fiction while the intimacy he'd promised would develop between them hadn't. Asking to end it had been futile. Turned out appearances mattered more than anything to *both* those men and ultimately Callum was every bit as controlling as her father. In the end she'd stopped asking. She'd acted. *Badly.*

'Well?' the too good-looking tower of a man right in front of her now prompted, somehow sensing her unsteadiness. 'How far are you willing to go to stop this?'

'As far as it takes.' She blinked away the shameful memories, furious with her weakness—for thinking about herself in this moment. Because this was about Ashleigh—and she completely understood her sister's inability to say 'no' to her father. She wouldn't let her sister endure more than the unfair pressure she'd already faced.

'What's *weird* is why *you* have to go to such icky lengths to get what you want,' she pushed back on him. 'What's so repellent about you that forces you to *buy* a bride?'

That slow, wide smile curved his lips. Apparently he wasn't shamed in the least by her acidic question.

'You tell me,' he invited softly, leaning closer still. 'How repellent do *you* think I am?'

Oh, he was so *very* arrogant. She refused to respond to such a blatantly outrageous diversion. 'You need to call the wedding off.'

'But won't your family—'

'Lose the hotel?' She shrugged. 'I don't care. Ashleigh isn't for sale.'

'Ashleigh,' he echoed calmly. 'She hasn't mentioned you to me.'

Of course her sister hadn't. Elodie was an outcast for deserting her 'perfect' husband and 'perfect' life. Her parents now lived as if she'd never existed. She and Ashleigh had only remained in touch online until Ashleigh had borrowed a friend's phone last night.

'No.' Elodie's words slowed as she registered that somehow Ramon Fernandez had moved even closer to her. 'She wouldn't have dared.'

Ashleigh couldn't disobey her father. Not yet. Elodie understood that too. She'd been the same for so long.

Ramon was serious now. Finally. 'Because you're a danger to the deal.'

'Yes.'

The startling blue of his eyes thinned as his pupils flared and she found herself sinking into their dark depths. The crackling sensation across her skin was so foreign it took her too long to realise what it was. Chemistry. Sexual chemistry. To her horror she realised her heat wasn't entirely comprised of rage at all. Her pulse thundered because this wasn't some tempting tendril of intimacy. This was an untrammelled cannonball of lust suddenly running amok within her. All because he was standing so close. It was something she'd never before felt. Instant. Intense. Completely and utterly inappropriate. Horrified at the utterly unbidden rush of want, she gasped sharply.

But the attraction was overpowering—and terrifyingly unstoppable.

'And you're a danger to me,' he whispered.

'Very much so.' She bluffed.

Because she knew now that the opposite was true—he was an absolute danger to her. But she couldn't seem to back away from him. She should. She should get away. She didn't need to test his measure. He thought and said and did what he wanted with no compunction and no remorse and certainly no consideration for another's feelings. And yet here she was, a heartbeat away from him.

'How, exactly?' he breathed.

That heat from deep within spread across every inch of her body and burned her skin. To her amazement a light flush echoed on his—colour scorching those angular cheekbones as his intense focus dropped to her mouth. With innate understanding she realised that he was considering kissing her. Instinctively her lips parted—that was to breathe, right? Because the shock stole her breath.

But she didn't step back. She refused to let him intimidate her. Because that's all this was—an attempt at intimidation. He was so sure of himself—enraptured with his own power—sensual and otherwise. But this close she caught a hint of his rich, oaky scent and the reason why she was even here at all began to slide from her mind as a shadowy, heated haze enveloped her. His long jet lashes lowered and suddenly his lips were but a whisper from hers.

With the last thread of resistance she remembered. Murmured, 'You would cheat on your fiancée so easily?'

His eyebrows flickered but he didn't pull back. 'You would betray your sister?'

'It's no betrayal,' she denied huskily. 'I've already told you I'll do *anything* to stop this marriage.'

She would put herself between him and her sister.

His lips twisted in triumph and he lifted his head away from her. His eyes glittered as he stared as she ran a tongue across parched lips. She realised that *he'd* been testing *her*. He hadn't *actually* intended to kiss her and that she felt *disappointment* was truly awful.

'You're not in love with her,' she accused bitterly.

'No,' he admitted with brutal candour.

Pain and fury and humiliation coalesced within her. How could he—and how could her parents—do this? Elodie wouldn't let them hurt Ashleigh in this way.

'So she's nothing but a toy?' she flared scornfully. 'A pawn in some bigger game you're playing? Just a thing to be sacrificed?'

'You think it would be so bad to be married to me?' he asked too mildly.

'Apparently I'm not the only one who thinks that, given the lengths you're having to go to get yourself a wife.'

His flash of amusement infuriated her all the more. How could he laugh? It was sickening.

'It's all about you,' she erupted. 'Your status. Your needs.'

'You don't think there'll be any benefits to her in the arrangement?'

'None that are worth it.' Not Ashleigh's innocence and liberty and dreams for her own future.

Elodie had long ago vowed never to get involved with another man again. She'd fought hard for her own freedom. She'd done horrible, necessary things. But she would suffer far more if it could save her sister from the same.

'For some unfathomable reason you want to get married,' she said. 'So perhaps it doesn't matter who the unfortunate woman is.'

He was unnervingly still, that intensity sharpening his eyes. 'You have another candidate in mind?'

Candidate. As if it were a job.

'Another poor soul, you mean?'

The devastating good looks of the man, his searing wealth, his callous lack of care and her own horrendously *animal* response to him fuelled her fury to the point where all control was lost.

'Sure,' she added acidly. 'If you want a wife so *desperately*, then you can marry *me*!'

CHAPTER TWO

JUAN RAMON FERNANDEZ clenched every muscle and made himself remain still. Not because he'd recoil but rather he was on the verge of pulling her against him and sealing the deal with an incendiary kiss!

But he did *not* want a wife. He would never *want* a wife. Yet the unpalatable truth hitting him hard was that he might very well *need* one. Soon. *That* was surely the only reason why he was almost overcome by the most inexplicable urge to grate out an expletive-laden acceptance of this fiery woman's scathing proposal. Why he'd haul her into his arms before she could change her mind. Why he had the impulse to carry her off to the nearest altar this instant—impossibly happy to! Because then he'd take her to bed.

Fortunately Elodie Wallace's very direct, very condemning blue gaze nailed him to the spot as that roar of possession swept through him.

Possession?

He'd been possessed. Momentarily gone mad.

Blinking, he spun and stalked to the gleaming glass counter in the corner behind his desk.

'Would you like a drink?' he asked unevenly.

He'd pour hers and swig directly from the bottle if it wouldn't betray his loss of composure. And he was damn well clinging to that facade with a death grip.

'I'm not leaving until you agree to release Ashleigh from this sham engagement.'

He splashed four fingers of whisky into a crystal tumbler before glancing back at the flame-haired fury standing in the centre of his study. She had guts, he'd give her that. Bold as anything and beautiful with it. A little thing with a big impact. The chandelier must have been dusted recently, or perhaps Piotr had changed the bulbs because the light illuminated her so intensely it was like she gleamed from the inside out. And when she shook her head at him, all fury and scorn, her mass of red hair glittered like a waterfall of fire across her shoulders. He couldn't look away from her if he tried. Which was a further loss of control he didn't appreciate.

Oh, who was he kidding? He *fully* appreciated looking at her. A human form tempest crossed with a Siren and right now he relished the distraction she was—mitigating the rage rising within. The fact was he had no power to release her sister from an engagement he was no part of. It was another arm of his family at fault. His *aunt*. Apparently not content with the company money she received, she was willing to use her own *son* to steal the most priceless jewel in the family treasure chest.

'I mean it,' Elodie-the-Beautiful declared defiantly, her hair catching the light as she tossed her head again.

Amusement rippled through him. Amusement that he didn't ordinarily indulge in. Amusement dangerously intertwined with lust and as inappropriate as hell given the situation. He sipped his drink—another thing he didn't ordinarily indulge in—hoping it would settle the *other* urges still rippling through him, but the burn wasn't enough to clear his head. He took another, deeper draw. Then he gave in and accepted that this was no ordinary day and he was going to have to do something drastic to resolve this.

'Piotr!' Ramon called loudly. 'Change of plan for this evening,' he said brusquely the second his assistant appeared, but he kept his gaze on Elodie. 'I'm staying in. Please send my apologies, prepare dinner for two and ensure the guest suite is ready.'

That amusement tightened as he watched her jaw slacken and then in a flash her entire body stiffened with fury again.

'The guest suite?' Her query dripped with iced loathing.

'Well, I thought it might be a little soon for my

room but I don't mind having you there tonight if that's what you'd prefer,' he purred.

He shouldn't have said it. Couldn't resist. Blamed the drink and set it down.

She stared open-mouthed at him. 'You're...'

Yeah. He had no words either right now. He could only inwardly curse.

Ramon would be the first to acknowledge that his regimented life could sometimes be boring, but his narrow focus was utterly deliberate. Greed—hunger for excess in *all* forms—was the family curse. His father had allowed his appetites to spiral out of control regardless of the cost to his family. Ramon had an equally rampant appetite, but he'd chosen to channel it into work. He'd relished the challenge of turning the family conglomerate he inherited too soon from overly stretched to stratospherically successful. Relationships were out. Never was he getting married. His father's rapacious genes ran through him, and he wasn't destroying any woman the way his father had destroyed his mother.

So the time Ramon offered a partner was limited. Anything long-term a definite no-go. And women didn't like coming second to work, didn't like that he travelled so much and never invited them along—so it was easy enough to keep emotional complication at bay. Nowadays on the rare occasions it got the better of him he slaked sexual hunger with a one-night stand. Maybe it had been a while. Maybe that was why when the door-bell had rung and he'd glanced at the security feed from the front door, he'd been intrigued by the bold woman staring straight into the camera. When she'd outlandishly claimed to be *his fian-cée's* sister, he'd simply had to indulge the ridiculous urge to let her in. He'd been unable to resist hearing what she'd wanted to say. Turned out to be quite a lot. By admitting little and encouraging her ire, he'd grasped what was really going on.

Her sister. His cousin. His aunt making a monstrous mistake.

So yeah, he was far from bored now as he watched Elodie's lusciously full lips press together, part, then press together again.

Still no words. Right.

A wash of colour betrayed her despite the immaculate make-up and to his horror he felt an answering wash of heat suffuse his own face. Again. He'd never heard of Elodie Wallace before now but he wished he had. Wished he'd been warned that when entering her orbit he'd have an intensely sexual reaction. Her eyes were a far more vibrant blue than his and right now they were very alert. Her slick make-up didn't entirely mask the freckles over her face but it was expertly done—her long lashes were enhanced, her lips shiny—while her slender figure was showcased to perfection with that stunning outfit. In theory her black pants suit would be appropriate for any occasion but the beaded bustier she wore beneath the blazer gave him a glimpse of her breasts almost spilling from the top and was sexy as hell. Dominatrix-lite. All she was missing was a riding crop. She was here to demand what she wanted and she wasn't leaving until she got it.

'You can marry me!'

Her outrageous suggestion hung in the air above him like a Shakespearean dagger. A dramatic temptation that a devil within still urged him to accept because it would so neatly solve the situation that he hadn't anticipated would come to a head so soon.

'You just said you weren't leaving until Ashleigh's freedom is secured.' He mastered the mess of emotions engulfing him and broke the scalding silence with as mild an expression as he could muster. 'I need time to consider my options. You may stay while I do that or you can leave.'

Ungallant as his deception was, he had to find out as much as he could from her and he could never confide to anyone—let alone a complete stranger—that his own family had their knives out and had caught him off guard.

'But if you do choose to leave,' he added, 'then the plan currently in place will likely continue.'

'You need *time*?' she echoed incredulously. 'It should take a man like you less than two seconds to realise dragging a teenager to the altar is a more than bad idea,' she snapped. 'Yet apparently, you're incapable of rational thought on this.'

She was right and she expected him to back down. She was used to getting what she wanted. Her confident diva aura was total demonstration of the fact. Curiosity devoured his brain—all he could think about was all the things he wanted to learn about *her*. Mostly inappropriate things. He gritted his teeth and summoned some self-control.

'Your kind offer of accommodation isn't really a *choice* for me, is it?' She stepped closer until she stood toe to toe with him. 'Does it make you feel good to exert control over someone?' she asked, her voice husky and low as she glared up at him irately. 'Is that what gets you going?'

He could only stand and stare at her. Couldn't let himself so much as breathe. Because *she* was what got him going in this instant and another acerbic challenge like that would have him slip the leash.

'Is that why you want a young bride?' she challenged further, oblivious to the storm brewing within him. 'Do you think you can mould her into your ideal wife?'

He didn't want to control her. He wanted to be consumed in her fire. He was so tempted to take her in his hands and tease her more. Instead he dragged in a steadying breath and harshly demanded *information*.

'Why wouldn't Ashleigh have dared mentioned you?'

Her eyes widened.

When he'd got this inappropriately close earlier, her haughty facade had fallen and he'd seen
an uncontrollable response flash—not fear but a
flare of attraction that mirrored his in every way.
Instant, unwanted, intense. A weakness. He saw it
again now and would exploit it. Because when she
was emotional she exploded and truth emerged.
He had to use those tactics because he didn't trust
her. Nothing personal. He didn't trust anyone, not
when he came from a family gored by infighting.
Not when his own father had been a master of betrayal. Not when he'd been forced to be complicit
in his old man's deceit.

He'd thought the worst of all that was in the
past. Thought he'd made enough amends on be-
half of his gluttonous father. Apparently not. He
knew his aunt Cristina had suffered as a spoiled
but ignored second child, as a young woman taken
advantage of by a man who'd consumed everything he could from everyone he encountered. But
that she would consider doing this?

He'd thought her interest in a hotel investment
in the South of England was little more than a van-
ity project for her son. He'd missed the off-paper
condition—a *wedding*.

That told him this wasn't about Elodie's family's barely-breaking-even hotel. This was about
his family's private island. The sanctuary his
mother had retreated to in her despair and which
had returned to the family trust since her death.

The trust decreed that lifelong occupancy rights were granted to the most senior male of the family as long as he were *married*. While Ramon was the most senior male, he was single. If the next in line—*Cristina's son*—were to marry, then *he* could claim occupancy—and development—rights. Ramon couldn't allow that to happen because Cristina would use her son to destroy everything Ramon's mother had built there.

Ramon could mount a legal challenge to amend the trust. Should've done that already, but since his mother's death he'd buried himself even more in work and somehow three years had passed. But Ramon would protect his mother's legacy by whatever means necessary—especially now he knew he no longer had the time for a protracted legal battle.

So he *did* need to know everything about the fire-breathing beauty before him. No way would his aunt allow a woman like Elodie Wallace to enter the family—which meant Cristina didn't know about her and that could play very well into his hands. Perhaps he was the one who'd take revenge this time. Maybe he'd finally make his aunt pay for the cruelty she'd shown his mother in her grief.

'Elodie?' He caved in to temptation and gently cupped her face. 'Are you persona non grata?'

She trembled slightly at his touch but she didn't

pull back. The hint of hurt crossed with courage in her eyes made his chest tighten.

Yes, he could save time, money and stress by getting married himself. The trust didn't specify that he had to *stay* married or for how long he even had to *be* married. Because in his hypocritical family, the concept of divorce supposedly didn't exist. But it would for him because there was no way in hell that he would ever marry for real. All he had to do was get married for long enough to invoke the occupancy rights. Maybe he would call Ms Elodie Wallace's bluff. Right now he wanted to do *that* more than anything.

'What did you *do*?' He provoked with a silkily patronising tone, pleased to see the instant flare in her eyes. 'What's really so dangerous about a little thing like you?'

'I lied.' She glared, finally goaded. 'I cheated. I abandoned my responsibilities.'

There was a ring of truth in her flash that he couldn't ignore.

'That bad, huh?' He tried to keep his tone light but his anger flared because he knew too well how those things damaged people. His father had lied, cheated. His mother had abandoned her responsibilities. And this woman was apparently every bit as fickle as she was beautiful and right now that pissed him off more than anything.

'Worse.' She was ferociously defiant.

'Yet here you are sweeping in to save your sister from a fate worse than death,' he snarled, because she was a contrary mix of shameless and protective.

'Because *she's* innocent.'

And Elodie wasn't. Bitterness burned. He could never, *ever* trust her. Which meant she presented one problem while being the solution to another in the one stunning package. He moved closer still, needing not just to see her reaction, but to feel it. He put his hand on her waist. A tremor instantly wracked her beautiful body, but she kept her head high, captivating *him* with her stormy gaze despite him being the one holding her. His smile was both twisted and unbidden. Without a doubt they would end up in bed together and he knew to his bones it would be mind-blowing. But that time was not now.

'Well, thank you for your honesty,' he muttered. 'It seems an appropriate time to admit that I haven't been completely forthcoming with you.'

And he still wasn't going to be entirely honest because some family secrets he could never tell. It didn't matter, she'd just admitted her prior deceit so she'd hardly care.

'*I'm* not the man intending to marry your sister,' he finally said softly. 'My cousin is.'

CHAPTER THREE

'PARDON?' ELODIE STARED at the stunning man as a rushing noise echoed in her head. She can't have heard him properly.

'My cousin is the man coercing your sister into marrying him. Well, actually, it's really his mother doing the coercing. My aunt.'

His *aunt*? She gaped. 'You're not Ramon Fernandez?'

'I am Juan Ramon Fernandez. You were seeking *Jose* Ramon,' he explained with a faintly regretful air. 'We are both known as Ramon.'

She suddenly realised he was still holding her and sharply pulled free of the hold that had been disconcertingly comforting. 'Not at all confusing.'

'The names are a family thing.' He watched her step backwards. 'My mother Daniela's family, actually. Fernandez is her name. The first Ramon was *her* father. My mother married a businessman who became CEO and took control of the Fernandez empire—continuing the family name through me was part of their deal. It is my mother's sister Cristina causing the problem. Her son—Jose Ramon Fernandez—is to marry Ashleigh.'

Stunned, Elodie tried to process all that information but it was almost as convoluted as one of her most challenging escape room clues.

Jose Ramon. Juan Ramon. Ramon. Both Fernandez.

She had it wrong. *This* man was not Ashleigh's prospective groom, that was someone else entirely—his cousin on his mother's side. And instead of doing the mental gymnastics to sort all that out, heat simply swamped her from head to toe as that illicit part deep within her pulsed with primal pleasure—

He wasn't the one. He wasn't taken. He could be hers.

Full mortification hit as she suppressed her own inner roar of possession. What was she *thinking*? She'd worked herself into a fury and she'd not even attacked the right guy and she should definitely *not* be so happy about it.

'You should have told me the moment you realised my mistake,' she growled.

He'd strung her along and allowed her to completely embarrass herself—hell, she'd all but thrown herself at the man in an attempt to show his immorality!

'I wanted to understand more about the situation—'

'You let me rage at you!' She couldn't restrain herself from raging again now. 'You let me—'

'You might have left before I could help.'

She paused, mistrustful as hell. 'You intend to help?'

'That surprises you?' His lips curved in that devastating smile. 'I think we may be able to resolve this situation to our best advantage if we work on it *together*.'

Best advantage? He spoke coolly, yet she felt an insidious warmth at the possibility of teaming up with him. But she couldn't lower her guard just because of his good looks and sudden charm. *This* Ramon was more than wealthy. He was powerful and definitely controlling. He'd just controlled the information he'd given her! He was used to being in charge—getting everything his way. And if he were anything like the controlling men she'd known, he wouldn't stand to be denied. She needed to be very, *very* careful. But she realised he'd given something away in admitting he'd wanted to understand more.

'You didn't know about the engagement plans,' she surmised.

He hesitated. 'No.'

'Yet you're this other Ramon's cousin?' Were they not close?

'Families can be complicated.' His gaze slid from her for the briefest second. 'I think Jose

Ramon is as much of a pawn as your sister. He won't stand up to either his mother or your father.'

She felt a flare of pity for Jose Ramon because she had the feeling he wouldn't have a snowball's chance in hell of standing up to *this* man either. She knew how hard it was to say no to powerful people. It had taken her years to develop the skill. 'How old is he?'

'An immature twenty-two.' He cocked his head. 'How old are you?'

She ignored his question. 'Why does your aunt want him married to my sister?'

He hesitated. 'Because I have no plans to marry and they know it.'

'What's the relevance of *your* relationship status?' she asked with blunt sarcasm.

Even though that greedy part within her was utterly, keenly interested.

'It's everything.' He regarded her with that shameless arrogance. 'In a family like mine marriage is rarely about love. It's about assets and heirs and continuity of control. Some of our property is held in trusts because it is always better for assets to remain within the family. Most of the wider family are happy to let me remain in charge and do all the work as long as they get their quarterly dividends. But there are always some who'll never have enough. Cristina will never have enough.' He drew breath. 'So the pressure will continue on poor Jose Ramon to marry—if not your sister then someone else because if he beats me up the aisle then he could gain control of one particular property portfolio.'

'So this is really all a fight within your own family.'

Which meant to some extent he was still to blame for this situation. Which was good because she felt safer being angry with him.

'There are warring family factions in every generation, no?' He shrugged negligently. 'Dysfunction is often the norm.'

'In ridiculously wealthy dynasties, perhaps. I wouldn't really know.' But that wasn't quite true. Her family was dysfunctional. They didn't have the assets and heirs but they certainly had the control issue. 'So what are you going to do?'

'Well, I am seriously considering your proposal.'

'My…' She stared at him fixedly as a rush of adrenaline deafened her again. *'What?'*

'Marriage is the one thing both our families want. Perhaps we should give it to them.'

'I was speaking *facetiously*.' Yet the raw attraction burgeoning inside begged to differ.

'Were you?' He moved closer to her again.

This was bad. When he was close her brain failed and her body burned.

'How disappointing,' he added softly. 'Let's revisit it as a realistic prospect to solve our respective problems.'

'*Our* problems?' Breathless, she retreated a step. 'Sounds like this is about *your* problems which I definitely don't need to be part of.' She took another step back. 'I should go—'

'Stop.' He grabbed her hand. 'Stay. Sit.'

It wasn't his words that stopped her, but the jolt at his touch. Not an electrical current but a shot of pure desire—instantly followed by rage. She desperately hauled back her composure. 'I am not a dog you can command,' she snapped.

He paused. 'Please.'

'Not much better.'

He smiled. She was immune to the charm of it. *Immune*. She was not being dictated to by any man ever again.

'An apology might go a little way to salvaging the situation,' she muttered.

He cocked his head as he studied her thoughtfully. Right. This man apologised to no one. He didn't admit mistakes. Too arrogant to believe he even made any. And this was fast becoming too much about her and her increasingly uncontrollable insane reaction to someone she knew would be so wrong for her.

She needed to get out of here. She would figure out an alternative solution. She would break Ashleigh out of there and bring her back to London, find another job to support them both. It would be hard, but they could survive on their own together. But Juan Ramon Fernandez still had

hold of her hand and somehow without her notic-
ing he'd stepped closer again and all she could
focus on was his finely tailored dinner jacket and
her itchy-fingered desire to discover the heat of
him beneath the starched white shirt.

'May I offer something even better,' he said
smoothly. 'It's getting late. It's been a stressful
evening. I get hungry when stressed. Do you? Stay
and have dinner. We'll talk. Swap family horror
stories—'

'And come up with an actually *practical* solution?' she interrupted.

For Ashleigh—only for Ashleigh—would she
even consider this. She would ignore his charming
and courteous side, stay on task, and she would
never let him railroad her into anything as ridiculous as marriage.

'Precisely. I can help your sister. And you.' He
gazed down at her. 'I have a couple of calls I need
to make. Would you like a moment to freshen up
while I do? Piotr will take you—'

'To the guest suite,' she muttered dryly. She was
not thinking about his comment about her staying
in *his* room. That had been way too much.

He smiled, unabashed. 'What do you say—will
you stay?'

Awareness of danger feathered across her skin
but the fact was she was short on time and ideas.
And as he seemingly didn't want his cousin and
Ashleigh's marriage either, she needed all the help

she could get to stop it. Plus she didn't want to show any kind of weakness in front of him. Running away would only reveal how much he got to her. His supposed interest in her stupid proposal was little more than a joke, but even if he was serious he'd have a change of heart once he knew more about the reputation she'd cultivated in the months after she'd run out on her marriage, when she was trying to force Callum into finally accepting their separation. But once Ramon got beyond the marriage idea, perhaps they could work together. She was wary of his power, but if he were on her side, then she maybe could use it.

'I'll stay for dinner,' she said haughtily. 'But only so we can sort out this situation to my satisfaction.'

'Perfect,' he muttered soothingly and released her hand.

Weirdly, walking away from the man made her shiver. She pulled her blazer together, annoyed by the absurdly certain feeling he would sort the situation. He was the capable kind who could sort anything and everything. Even more annoying was her attraction to him. For a moment she imagined sweeping along in this velvet atmosphere wearing some gorgeous dress. Imagined being alone with Ramon Fernandez any time she felt like it. Imagined the confidence to do anything she wanted. With him. *To* him…

The effort to redirect *those* thoughts came at a

cost. With every step away from him an almost blinding headache came on swiftly and strongly. Thankfully the immaculately efficient Piotr opened a door, then stood back to let her through.

'I'll be back in about twenty minutes to escort you to the dining room,' he said.

'Thank you.'

She leaned back against the door the second she closed it. Ashleigh's safety was the most important thing—the *only* thing to focus on right now.

She stared at the enormous bed—more luxurious than any hotel perfection. Not that she'd ever stayed in one of the hotels in the Fernandez empire though. Another fantasy engulfed her—of being in his room. That shocking comment had been pure temptation. Her face flamed and she chastised her wayward imagination. Her head pounded, exacerbated by not eating in hours because she'd been too nervous about her mission. And now the riot of her wholly unexpected and inappropriate response to him caused even more inner tension, resulting in a fierce pounding at her temples. She staggered into the stunning bathroom, dampened a cloth and went back to sink into the large armchair beside the bed. Closing her eyes, she pressed it to her face, desperate to relax.

Ramon tensed, his gaze narrowing on the screens in front of him that were mirroring those of two of his highly paid personal assistants who were working late in the city office. He was juggling calls with both.

'I want to see everything that's there. Go back further.'

His assistant immediately obliged, knowing better than to question, no matter how exceptional or unusual these particular instructions were.

He'd already skimmed the plans for the island that Cristina and Jose Ramon had commissioned and planned to submit for local government approval the second Jose Ramon had occupancy. Yet instead of prioritising that imminent disaster he'd fallen down the rabbit hole that was Elodie Wallace's social media profile. So *many* party pictures—not yachts and private beaches and the like—this was all clubs and bars in the city.

'There's nothing earlier,' his assistant said.

Nothing prior to the sudden rush of pictures starting about three years ago. Furthermore, the flurry of party girl activity had been updated only sporadically in the past year. Her profile picture showed her standing between two other women who looked to be a similar age. Her squad? A curvy brunette and an arctic-looking blonde. They made a stunning trio, but it was the flame-haired vixen in the centre who he couldn't help staring at. Who he felt absurdly angry about.

It didn't bother him that she'd mistaken him for his cousin. He wasn't insulted by her assumption that he would marry someone so young and who he barely knew. No, that wasn't the problem. *She* was. Specifically, his reaction to her. Her wild red hair, striking blue eyes and temperamental sass sharpened his senses. The strength with which she drew him was beyond irritating. It was her unexpected appearance, right? She'd stormed into his home—dressed to thrill—and demanded what she wanted.

So yeah, she'd got his attention. That was all. Because for years now he'd proven to himself that he was not his father. That he *didn't* have that bastard's age-old weakness for a beautiful woman. That he wouldn't ever be controlled by base urges in the way his repellent old man had been.

Ramon was better than that. Only now, in mere moments, that belief was destroyed. One look at her and he'd been stupefied. One conversation and he was almost tongue-tied. His animal instinct urged him to capture and claim. He'd been unable to resist the desire to touch her.

'She works for an escape room company,' the other assistant informed him. 'She's a hostess there.'

'Hostess?'

'You know, the one who reads the rules and then locks people in.'

And watches them try to worm their way out? Yeah. That made sense. He had the feeling she would enjoy that power trip. She liked to be in control.

'She was married.' His first assistant coughed. 'And is now divorced.'

His blood iced as the certificates appeared on the screen in front of him. 'Can you find anything about the ex?'

'Same town addresses. Presumably someone local. Looking at him now.'

There was a pause while his assistant typed.

'They went to the same school,' she said.

She'd married her high school sweetheart? Had she outgrown him? Broken his heart?

Ramon clicked the certificates away. Now he knew what she'd meant with her dramatic declaration—

I lied. I cheated. I abandoned my responsibilities.

He gritted his teeth. The details didn't matter. He didn't need to know anything more than the bare fact that she'd betrayed her husband. Leopards didn't change their spots.

His father had cheated on his mother many times and lied about it for years before making Ramon complicit in betrayal too. His father had tried to convince him that it was 'normal'—that Ramon would understand as he grew older. That they were very alike. And yes, Ramon looked like his father, worked like his father and had now long been stained by his father's sins.

He'd tried to protect his mother from the truth. Not only had he failed in that, she'd never forgiven him for his silence, assuming he'd known about the one betrayal that had been so much worse than Ramon could have ever imagined. His parents' marriage had been such a travesty, Ramon was never entering one of his own. At least not for real and not for long. Fortunately, Elodie had already proven that vows didn't signify to her. Which meant the impulsive solution aired earlier might actually have legs. She'd offered herself, had she not? She would do anything for her sister. What was a little agreement—a signature here and there?

'There's no mention of her on her parents' social media profiles,' his other assistant said. 'It's as if she doesn't exist.'

Irritated, he snapped, 'And her sister?'

'Doesn't seem to be online.'

Which was weird. But Elodie's social media profile was easily accessible. Beautiful Elodie in short, form-fitting dresses—all seductive smiles, drinks in hand, nightclubs, restaurants and parties. Unsurprisingly she was accompanied by a vast assortment of men. Apparently disowned by her parents, she was a wild child. And an appallingly base part of him was pleased that Elodie Wallace knew how to have a good time.

'Enough. Thank you.' He ended the calls and remained staring at the screen full of pictures for far too long.

She would be able to hold her own with him.

She was as uninterested in happy ever after as he was. She was about immediate gratification. His competitive nature surged. No one would give her a good time in the way he would. He would have her resplendent in his bed, mindless with bliss, with nothing other than sighs tumbling from her tart mouth. Because that was the element missing in all these photos. His gut instinct told him her pleasure here was superficial amusement at best. Not bone-deep satisfaction.

So maybe he would thwart his aunt and get the occupancy rights of the property the moment before she thought she'd succeeded. And in the same sweep, he would enjoy an affair with the enthusiastic and experienced Elodie Wallace.

He finally stalked along the corridor to the guest suite, anticipating her annoyance that it was more than an hour since Piotr had shown her to the room, not a mere twenty minutes. That it was Ramon himself coming to fetch her for dinner, not his man. In part he'd wanted to test whether she'd skip out or not. He knocked on the door but got no response. Opened it and paused. She was reclined in the large armchair, a flannel folded across her eyes—was she asleep?

He moved forward, not expecting that she'd be so relaxed as if she were having a spa session at a hotel. But of course, she was a confident queen. He crouched before her. Her satiny skin tempted as did her soft-looking mouth. But there was something vulnerable in her positioning.

'Elodie.' His whisper came out gruff and he had to clear his throat.

She lifted away the cloth and looked straight into his eyes. The cloth must've been damp because much of her make-up was removed and she was disturbingly pale.

'Oh. I'm...' She made to sit up.

He frowned and pushed her back against the chair. 'You have a headache?'

'I probably look like a racoon.'

But the shadows beneath her eyes weren't streaks of mascara. She looked wary and sensitive. Interesting given her boldness earlier.

'What time is it?' She bit her lip.

'I took longer than I'd thought. Wasn't sure you'd have stayed to be honest. Turns out you're lying here looking like death.' He studied her curiously. 'Been burning the candle at both ends?'

Had she been out partying and just not updating her social media?

He heard a defiant little hitch of her breath.

'Of course, that's how I like it,' she said.

'So you have no problem sleeping wherever and whenever?' And with whomever?

He shouldn't care about that. Her past was the past and none of his business. But without doubt *he* would be her immediate future.

'Right.' She lowered her lashes but beneath

them her eyes gleamed. 'It's a skill I've perfected over the years.'

'Impressive.' As was the coy death look she was shooting him now.

He watched her pull herself together before him—in two blinks she morphed back into the confident woman who'd coolly knocked down his front door. Her lashes lifted and she looked at him directly. The ambient temperature soared. Colour surged back beneath her skin. Her blush was a giveaway reaction to him that was completely beyond her control. As was his. This chemistry needed to be burned. He rose from his haunches and offered his hand. There was a small hesitation—as if she were bracing—before she took it. He locked his fingers firmly around hers—also inwardly bracing to contain his insane satisfaction—and tugged, helping her to her feet in a smooth movement.

Now they stood too close and still she met his gaze with that daring, fiery defiance. The bed beckoned. He watched, waited. Would she make the move? She was definitely sexually interested. No way was he wrong about that. Which meant any moment now she'd lift her chin and press her lips to his. He wanted her to. Badly.

But she didn't. She'd frozen as if paralysed by the crackling reaction between them. His pulse thudded—pushing him to close the gap. Resisting the urge took almost everything he had.

'I'm hungry,' she said huskily.

He dragged in a breath. She was *very* good.
But this vixen had entered *his* den and he wasn't
afraid to engage with her. He wasn't bored anymore either. No, now they would spar. 'Then come
with me.'

CHAPTER FOUR

ELODIE HAD LITTLE choice but to accompany Ramon Fernandez down the corridor, given he didn't release her hand. Her pulse lifted, her breathing quickened and amazingly the pain in her head receded. She told herself it wasn't from his touch but rather the rush of adrenaline that his appearance had induced.

Okay, it was his touch, and she was completely out of her depth. But if he knew how much he affected her that would give him power, and Elodie never wanted anyone to have power over her again. Not emotional. Not physical. Not financial. She'd worked too hard for too long to gain her independence and her confidence. So she'd pull on her cool.

Once more she regretted coming here alone, but she'd never imagined that he'd be so attractive. She had to shake off this sense of intimacy that had deepened by virtue of him catching her resting. *Physical* distance would help but the house made that difficult. The dark colour scheme flowed into the dining room where the silverware gleamed in flickering candlelight. It was atmospheric and something smelled so good her mouth watered.

He released her hand and held a chair for her. 'Eat.'

Right now she was too hungry to think of a comeback to savage his tendency to command. Desperate to haul her scattered wits together, she did as he'd suggested and focused on the food. She would refuel her brain and then get it together.

Piotr presented the plates and then left. Salmon fillet, baby potatoes, a pretty salad—Elodie felt healthier just by looking at it. At the first mouthful she suppressed a moan. Exceptionally cooked, it wasn't rich and decadent but light and refreshing and everything she needed. She basically inhaled it. Maybe she ought to make polite conversation, but it was too hard to keep her emotions contained. Fortunately, he too seemed intently focused on stabbing the food with jerky movements. They both drank water, steering clear of the wine. Slowly she felt fortified, and by the time they moved to the elegant and refined fruit and cheese platter with an exquisite assortment of petit fours that she simply couldn't resist, she thought she might be able to handle anything.

'Better?' he asked quietly.

'Yes.' She finally dared to look at him directly and breathed in deep because it was a mistake.

He was appallingly handsome, but it was that

combination of alert amusement and awareness in his eyes that minced her brain again.

'When did you find out about Ashleigh's engagement?' he asked.

'Last night.'

'You've been kept out of the loop as much as I have,' he noted softly. 'Save your sister. Marry me.'

'That's crazy,' she muttered.

The crazy thing was that she was *tempted*—purely because of her physical response to him. Her whole body was on high alert. Sex had never been a big part of her life before, so this desire was shocking and diabolical and extremely difficult to control.

'Isn't accosting someone in their own home also crazy?' he said. 'Especially when you got the wrong guy. Perhaps impulsive is a better word. Perhaps we could impulsively marry.'

'Absolutely not.'

His smile flashed. 'Are you not attracted to my brilliance? My billions? Not even my body?'

She squirmed like a fish on a hook. 'None of the above.'

'You lie a lot.'

'Your ego is astronomical.' She sipped more water. 'I don't need to create more problems for myself by entering a foolish and unnecessary marriage. Two wrongs do not make a right. And frankly, I don't believe that you really feel forced into doing something so drastic.'

'Unfortunately my aunt's duplicity forces me into action of some kind,' he said mildly. 'Cristina wants assets. I imagine she wants Jose Ramon to produce the Fernandez heir for the next generation. As I'm pushing thirty and don't have three offspring already, she hopes that I'm a lost cause and so—'

'I'm *never* having your baby.' This talk of heirs and offspring shocked her into interrupting him.

He just laughed. 'Indeed you are not. I have zero intention or desire to procreate.'

'Right. Good.'

'As we agree so easily on this, I'm confident we'll find more common ground.' He smiled, all smug confidence. 'Our marriage may well be an oasis of emotional calm.'

She stared at him incredulously.

'I will retain control of the Fernandez empire,' he said.

That's when she saw the glint of steel and realised he was lethally serious.

'But if you're without an heir—what happens then?' she asked.

'I'll ensure the succession plan is in the best interests of the company but I need to buy a little time first. Getting married is the most expedient way of achieving that.'

'But you don't need to marry *me* at all. You could marry anyone.'

'Of course I could,' he agreed.

Elodie stilled, shocked as a hot spear of jealousy stabbed deep inside her.

'But that wouldn't solve the problem within *your* family,' he added with a charming smile. 'Won't your father simply find your sister another husband she doesn't want?'

That was a *horrible* possibility.

'You need a more permanent solution for your own family drama,' Ramon said. 'I can be that solution.'

He made it sound so simple. So easy to say yes to something so insane. But Ramon Fernandez was more powerful than both her father and her ex put together, and she should be running far, far away.

'I've been married before,' she said flatly. 'I have zero intention of doing it again.'

He leaned back and studied her. 'You were nineteen.'

She glared at him. He *knew*?

'Why did it end?'

The atmosphere sharpened. When did he learn that about her—had he pried into her personal life while she'd been resting?

'You were unfaithful?' he asked harshly.

'Repeatedly,' she lied furiously.

His expression pinched. He believed her. It was

important that he did. It was another layer of armour for her. She *needed* him to think she was trouble—that she was tough. That he couldn't control her.

'Which I assume is the source of your supposed danger,' he said. 'Your flightiness. Your high *needs*. Perhaps our marriage could restore your reputation?'

'I don't want to *restore* my reputation,' she snapped. 'I *like* my life. It took a lot to get my freedom and I'll fight to keep it however I have to—'

'You do realise that I'm not talking about forever?' he interrupted with a low drawl.

'You do realise that I could make your married life the worst thing ever?'

'I was rather hoping you'd suggest that.' His smile widened to full crocodile threat. 'You're everything they'd hate. My marrying you would be their worst nightmare.'

Great. Good to know her efforts to be repellent had been so successful. She breathed through the hit and pulled on a ruthless smile—drawing on the persona she'd cultivated after walking out on her marriage after only five months. The one that had finally given her ex the impetus to agree to the divorce he'd tried to delay. He'd begged her to come back but never *listened* to why she didn't want to. He'd wanted the obedient Elodie he'd first met, not the free Elodie she'd desperately needed to be.

'Because I'm a troublemaker?'

She'd played 'unfaithful wife'. Repeatedly. She'd posted 'incriminating' pictures all over social media until finally neither Callum nor her father could stand the continued public humiliation. The divorce had been expedited at last, and Elodie had been wiped from her own family's photos.

And Ramon Fernandez clearly thought he knew all about her now—knew her fickleness, flippancy, infidelity. Of course he wasn't afraid of it. Maybe the only thing that mattered to him was money.

'Because you're an independent woman who's not afraid to say what she thinks or to ask for what she wants,' he corrected.

Elodie's breath stalled as a lick of pleasure curled inside her. Independent? Not afraid? Maybe he was just being smooth but that was how she wanted him to see her. Strength mattered. And she would remain strong in front of him now.

'Unfortunately that's not going to work on my side.' She coolly denied him. 'Because *you're* not *my* family's worst nightmare.'

'No?'

Hell, no. Her father, so impressed by grandeur, by supposed social standing, would be a drooling sycophant should he ever meet *this* Ramon Fernandez.

'You supposedly have billions,' she said. 'If I were to marry you they'd be over the moon, basking in the glory of such a connection. They wouldn't care if you treated me badly. In fact they'd probably cheer you on.'

His mouth thinned. 'Which is why—when the time is right—you'll give me hell and walk out. You'll destroy me like you no doubt destroyed that other guy.'

She masked her flinch. 'As if *you* would ever allow yourself to be destroyed.'

'You see?' The crocodile smile returned. 'It's perfect. Because you do not care about marriage. You do not care about me. Neither of us will mistake this for anything more than a temporary deal to resolve family drama.' He leaned close. 'You're as bulletproof as I am.'

He was so wrong. But she couldn't ever admit that to him.

'As appealing as you've made it sound,' she said with a bored expression, 'there's not enough in it for *me*.'

'No?' His gaze sharpened. 'Then tell me, Elodie Wallace, what is it that I can do for you?'

She fought to keep her brain together and not let the new sensual ache in her body derail her completely. 'Are you really trying to offer me anything I want in return for my hand in marriage?' She shook her head and went full bluff. 'Sorry, but I already *have* everything I want.'

'No,' he scoffed. 'There's something you need. There's always something.'

'You're saying anyone can be bought?' she asked.

He was so cynical.

'You know it.' He suddenly leaned close, his blue eyes glinting and jaw angular as he sucked in a sharp breath. 'Why not take everything that you can get from this?'

'"This"?'

'Don't pretend to be so naive,' he muttered harshly. 'Don't avoid the obvious.'

She couldn't believe the fire now in his gaze and couldn't stand the energy coursing through her. She had to move. She pushed back from the table at the exact moment he did. He moved with such rapid force the chair toppled behind him but he didn't care—he grabbed her hand instead.

People shook hands in all kinds of settings so the smallest of strokes of his thumb on her wrist shouldn't have had the effect on her that it did. But it was such a gentle caress. One he repeated—almost as if he were unconscious of the action. Except he was as aware of it as she. *Hyper*aware. Heat flooded her face and the answering splash of colour on his upper cheekbones melted her.

'*This* is the obvious?' Her voice was high and thin because she was breathless and yearning and hotter than she'd ever felt in her life.

'Has been from the moment you stormed my house.' He kept those mesmerising blue eyes on her. 'The fact is you want me as much as I want you.'

He crowded closer but she craved closer still. With a hitch of her breath, with an unconscious sway towards him she admitted it. *Invited*. His other hand landed on the small of her back—beneath her blazer. Her breasts tightened against her bodice. She gazed up at him, her lips parting as he lowered his head to hers. One kiss. Just one. Just to see.

He caught her mouth with his and in seconds it was the most sexually explicit kiss she'd ever experienced. His tongue teased then plundered, full of intent and carnal temptation. With a moan she sank against him, and his hold tightened. She gasped as his lips trailed lower, teasing the sensitive skin of her neck. Her knees weakened at the caress—such was the cliché she'd become. But in an instant she was his plaything. Somehow her blazer slipped from her shoulders to the floor. She swayed, so supple for him, so eager for his touch, and he lowered her back against the table. Their empty plates were at one end but now she was the dish on offer. And he feasted. His body was like rock and the intensity of *his* arousal turned her on even more. She was breathless with awareness of it—*ached* for it. She wanted him. Completely.

In moments they were hurtling towards a foregone conclusion. She would sleep with him. She would do *anything* with him. Frankly, he'd seduced her before even touching her and now that he had, she'd gone up in flames. Eviscerated. Inevitable. He tugged her bodice down. She sucked in a shocked breath because he was strong and bold. Her breasts were exposed to his gaze, touch, tongue, and he took quick advantage in that order.

'You are stunning, my flame-haired vixen,' he groaned huskily. 'You know how to make an impression and I so appreciate it.'

'It wasn't for you,' she moaned.

'I know,' he laughed exultantly. 'But I'm not my cousin. I'm not a weak man. I know what I want and I'm not afraid to reach for it.'

He wanted *her* and he made no effort to hide it. No effort to restrain his intense kisses, caressing her with mouth and hands and closeness—rousing her to an equally wild hunger.

This boiled down to *sex*. From the moment she'd set eyes on him the awareness had kicked in. It had been a swift, unstoppable reaction she'd never experienced before and incited a shocking greed that she couldn't control. She wrapped her leg around his hips so she could feel his hardness right where she was aching and wet. Even through the layers of clothes, the feel of him against her was shudderingly good. He moved against her again and again in the most delicious erotic tease and suddenly she was about to lose control. She was about to—

'Oh, no,' she muttered to herself, a shocked gasping whisper. *'No!'*

'But you're so close,' he muttered hotly. 'Let

me finish you—' He broke off on a growl and stepped back.

Elodie almost wept as a wave of frustration smacked into the empty space he'd left. She'd be shaking in bliss if she'd just bit her lip! For a split second longer she remained leaning back on the dining table, staring up at him. The fire in his eyes, the flush on his cheeks, the satyr-like smile on his lips...he gazed down at her so hungrily and she was stunned at how sexy *she* felt. She'd been more turned on in the last minutes than she'd ever been in her life—a breath from an orgasm she'd never experienced with another.

And it had taken him mere moments. A chill ran through her body, dousing the flame of desire. That had been too intense. Too quick. She scrambled to cover up. She'd never been as close to losing complete control of herself.

'Games, Elodie?' he growled softly. 'Of course you like to play them. But you really don't need to feign shyness.'

She wasn't playing anything, but she would let him think it while she got her head together. She needed the protection of his disapproval. If he knew how shaky and vulnerable she actually was right now, she'd be completely at his mercy.

'I'll happily play whatever games you want once we're married.' Ramon curled his hands into fists, striving to regain control of himself.

She'd surprised him by slamming on the brakes,

but he'd seen the keening ache still in her expression as she'd turned away to tug the bustier back in place. He picked up her little blazer. She snatched it off him with trembling hands.

'This has been a waste of time.' She flipped her hair free and it settled in wild disarray across her shoulders.

'It has not,' he retorted, folding his arms across his chest to stop himself grabbing her back against him. 'But unlike you, I'm not one for making dramatic declarations, I'll actually *do* whatever is necessary to resolve this. The question is, will you? Or are you all talk and no action?'

'I'm taking action. By leaving. Now.'

He didn't want that, but he clamped down on his urge to restrain her with brute force. 'Running away because you can't handle the temptation?'

Twin spots of colour flooded her cheeks. She almost looked prim. 'You really think you're that irresistible?'

'I really think this chemistry is,' he threw back at her.

She stilled, stared at him with wide, wild blue eyes.

'I'm not afraid to be honest,' he growled. 'Seems you need a little more practice.'

But doubt sliced—was this just strong chemistry or was it those more *unfortunate* genetic tendencies unleashed? Ramon had vowed never to come unhinged by lust. Yet here was his very personal challenge to that. So he would show restraint. Just to prove to himself that he could—that he wasn't like his father in everything.

'Piotr will drive you home,' he said roughly. 'I'll be in touch tomorrow. We'll solidify the plan.'

'Make an actual proper plan, you mean.'

He watched her worry her lip—that's all it took to reignite the need to pull her close. He definitely wasn't alone in feeling this, but he'd slow them down and ensure this would be a controlled explosion geared to extract maximum benefit for them both.

'I guarantee that if you marry me, your sister will be released from that engagement immediately,' he said. 'And you need this to be immediately, no?'

She didn't reply, which was better than an outright refusal. He sensed she was unsettled from something more profound than the insanity of this rash proposal. He got to her. It pleased him. It made them even.

'Thank you for dinner.' She ground out the most reluctant polite goodbye ever.

He laughed. She looked angry.

'My pleasure.' He should step back. Instead, he couldn't resist temptation again. Not when she stood there so defiantly—wordlessly daring him.

One kiss. Just one more. He bent and brushed his mouth gently against hers and felt the instinctive cling of her lips to his. No denial. She couldn't. Suppressing a guttural groan, he allowed himself another taste of her exquisite softness. He cupped her face to stop himself from searching out her curves but then he couldn't resist pressing her against the wall with his body. She melted like wax against him, and damned if that wasn't every bit as good as earlier. If not even better than the raging inferno of the straight-to-orgasm encounter they'd almost had on his dining table. She was so warm. So tender. So sweet. And with another swipe of his tongue the inferno was back. He growled and ground against her—torn between keeping his head and indulging his rampant appetite. He should just take her to bed. Slake this hunger. If he asked now she would say yes. But he wanted her acceptance of something so much more.

He tore his lips from hers, leaning back to study her. Her eyes were still closed as if she was lost in the moment. As if she'd never been kissed like that in her life. And maybe it made him a fool, but he was willing to go with it because he hadn't had a kiss like that either.

'I can hardly wait till we're married,' he muttered.

Her eyes opened and looked huge—dazed. Her bold, sexy clothes and her trembling, flushed response were a study in contrasts and he decided then that he would truly take his time because her surrender would be all the more satisfying.

'We're not getting married.'

'Sure we are. That's the only way I'll give you what you want.' He would convince her properly tomorrow. He would find her weak spot, apply pressure and win.

'Sleep on it. If you can,' he challenged softly. 'I'm not going to. I'm going to lie awake all night thinking about you. Specifically what I'm going to *do* with you the second I have that band on your finger.'

CHAPTER FIVE

'YOU HAVE ONLY one hour to escape!' With dramatic effort Elodie closed the heavy door on the group of excited pre-teens and turned the lock with a loud flourish.

Her first customers were making the most of the air-conditioning to escape the suffocating heat that London could shock with in the summer. By the time she got back to reception, Bethan had arrived and was sewing final touches onto a prop for the new scenario they had planned.

'You okay?' Bethan's eyes narrowed on her. 'You look tired.'

'Just a bit distracted.' Elodie smiled to cover up. 'I'm going to work from the back office for a while, can you monitor those guys?'

'Of course.' Bethan nodded. 'I'll bring you coffee shortly.'

Elodie hugged her as she went past. 'You're the *best*.'

Try though she might, Elodie couldn't stop thinking about Ramon Fernandez. Already in sleep deficit after the disturbed night before, worrying about Ashleigh, she'd lain awake for the whole of last night as well—thinking about *him* instead of trying to find alternative solutions to help her sister. She was pathetic. But she still couldn't process what had happened between them.

Lust. Instant. Rampant. Undeniable lust.

Seemingly a normal thing for him but an absolute first for her. Most of the time she didn't think about sex, and she tried not to think about her ex-husband Callum at all. Their physical relationship had been unsatisfying at best and in truth she wasn't anywhere near as experienced as people believed. All her nightclub party pictures had been for show to provide the humiliating evidence she needed for her liberation. So the uncontrollable moments in Ramon Fernandez's home last night?

Shocking. Even more shocking, was her appetite for more.

Bethan appeared in the doorway of the office but with no coffee in hand. Instead, she had a curious expression on her face. 'Someone's here to see you. He says it's a personal matter?'

Elodie stared at Bethan, then swivelled to check the CCTV displays that showed all the escape rooms, plus the reception area. They'd barely been open ten minutes and here he was—tall, *devious* and handsome.

'Lock him in the Prohibition room,' she said softly.

'Did you say *lock* him in?' Bethan checked, startled. 'Um… I don't think he's a customer. He—'

'Deserves it,' Elodie said flatly.

'Right. Uh, I'll get him in there right away then.' Bethan backed out of the office. 'I'll stay on reception to handle those others and the next scheduled.'

Elodie clicked a few commands on the audio-visual set-up to block the Prohibition room from Bethan's monitor on reception, then switched her own view to full-size on that very room. It was only a moment before the door opened and Ramon strolled in with that relaxed, yet predatory, ruler of the universe way of his. Bethan quickly closed the door without saying a word to him.

Elodie activated the intercom system. 'You have one hour to escape.'

'Elodie.' He slowly turned a full circle in the centre of the room, his alert gaze taking in the vibrant decor. 'I am locked in?'

'That is the point of an escape room,' she said acidly.

'You think I came here to play?' He stared straight into the CCTV camera that was mounted on the wall.

'Consider it a test.'

'What happens if I fail your test?'

She'd put him in the hardest of the escape rooms. Whole teams of people struggled to work the challenges out. She was certain he'd fail. 'Then I know you're not fit for purpose.'

He smiled. 'Are you not going to give me the rules—don't I get some sort of scenario I have to work through?'

Yeah, she'd skipped the three-minute spiel she usually gave before that final line.

'How can I pass your test if it's unfair from the outset?' he added.

She gritted her teeth. 'The year is 1922. It's the Prohibition era in the States, but you're a play-boy—running with the wrong crowd and trying to be a big man bootlegger. You've been lured to The Redhead, a speakeasy with a secret entrance beneath a barbershop, and locked in to be caught. If you're found here you'll forfeit your family fortune. You need to find the hidden mechanisms that will turn the basement bar back into a store-room and then make your escape before the police catch you.'

'Did you just say I've been lured to a redhead?' His mouth twitched. 'You really do like playing games…'

'It's the name of the bar.'

Elodie put on the jazz music that signalled the start of the hour. She watched him read all the supposedly 'random' notes on the counter and take note of the patterns painted on the walls. It took him only a moment to find the 'hint' envelope stashed behind one of the decorative bottles.

'Need help so soon?' she murmured.

'I want to get out of here as fast as possible.' He speed-read the letter inside. 'An interesting job you have, watching people struggle to work out the clues. The diversions, red herrings, complications. Do you enjoy seeing them sweat?'

She did want to see him sweat, actually. 'What do you think that says about me?'

'That you like to play but you keep yourself safe. Distanced.'

'I offer assistance when required.'

'Benevolence?' His laugh was low. 'No, you just like to display your superior intellect.'

'Not superior,' she countered. 'I have the advantage only because I know the rooms inside and out.'

'Because you designed them. You've set this trap for me.'

She watched him unlock the first cabinet and gritted her teeth. He was too quick. He was going to do this in less than an hour. 'You've been doing your research.'

'I stayed up all night finding everything I could about you.'

'That would hardly have taken all night,' she said uncomfortably. What did he think he knew now?

'The night was very hard.' He grinned. 'Will

you give me extra time given my performance
might be impaired due to the lack of sleep you
caused?'

'No.'

'I won't forget that small lack of mercy, Elodie. Maybe there'll come a time when I show you
no mercy.' He stood still and stared directly into
the camera. 'Here's the deal. When I escape this
room—in less than an hour—you'll elope with
me.'

Even though there were walls between them,
she felt that look burn through her. 'You're not really in a position to make demands.'

'I have copies of your parents' accounts,' he
said softly. 'You're going to want to see them.'

Her stomach dropped. 'How bad are they?'

'Can't say right now, I'm concentrating on de-
coding this cipher.' He pushed a series of buttons—in the right order. The cloth providing a
colourful backdrop for the musicians' platform
fluttered, swallowed into a small gap in the floor
and leaving a bland basement wall exposed.

'Oh, that's impressive,' he commented.

Elodie refused to feel pleasure at the praise. She
clicked to another screen and adjusted the temperature of the air conditioning. Willing to play
dirty to win.

Only a few moments later Ramon removed his
jacket, put it on the wooden table and rolled up

his sleeves. 'I appreciate your efforts to make this even more difficult for me.'

He flexed his hands and stepped forward to line up a series of cocktail glasses.

'*Copa de balón...*' He angled his head and read the gin bottles. Understanding he needed to read the colours in the mirror to input them in the right order. 'This business is for sale. The owner wants to retire. Meaning your job is potentially at risk. His asking price is steep.'

Elodie froze, hating him.

'It must be disappointing that you don't have the money to scrape together a bid when you're the one who's made such a difference to the bottom line with rooms like this and thus have inflated that asking price,' he added. 'You've brought in another stellar worker and everything. It must be nice to work with a friend. Bethan, right? The brunette on reception. She's in some of your social media photos.' He ran his hand over the knobs and lined them up. 'Wouldn't it be a shame if she lost her job too?'

'I'm not going to let that happen.'

'No? But the business leases this building and that's also coming up for renewal shortly. What if the landlord decides to sell? A new building owner might want to do something else with the space given it's such a central location. It could even be a good boutique hotel.' He paused. 'All that could be avoided if *you* were to buy the business.'

Elodie turned the audiovisual feed off completely. It was a calculated risk but one she had to take given he was at the three-quarter mark already. She ran down the secret fire escape passage to the compartment that was about to be flipped into the room and stepped onto the small space just in time. She heard the creak as the mechanism started. Lifting her chin, she pressed back as she was swung around on the small platform and into the room. Because what had been a shelf in front of him was now a hollow holding Elodie herself.

She met his stunned gaze with a defiant glare.

'*Wow*...' Ramon pressed his hand to his chest. 'Quite the jump-scare.' He regarded her with wide eyes as she stepped into the centre of the room. 'You really do know how to make an entrance. Here was me thinking the object of the exercise was to get *out* of the room.'

'There are surprises for the clients,' she muttered. 'Sometimes a mannequin, sometimes a fake skeleton—'

'Sometimes a beautiful woman.' He put his hands on her waist and pulled her flush against him. 'This is definitely an interactive experience. I—'

'Think you're done?' She stood stiffly against him.

'Yes.'

'No,' she said with some pleasure. 'It was a false finish.'

He stilled. 'So we're still locked in here?'

'You are. I can get out anytime I like.'

He gazed down at her, taking in her floor-length black skirt and high-necked fitted black shirt with its long row of pearl buttons. 'So are you a Victorian widow or scandalous witch? Either way, I like it.' He looked back into her face, his own half smile all mockery. 'I'm not sure you should have joined me in here, *cariño*.'

Elodie summoned all her strength to resist him. 'I'm not afraid of you.'

'I'm glad to hear it,' he said softly. 'I'm not afraid of you either.' He glanced into her eyes. 'Much.' He cupped her face and muttered quietly, 'Who's monitoring the cameras?'

'I turned them off.'

He stared at her for a long moment. 'Always three steps ahead, aren't you Elodie?'

She stared back at him silently.

'You want to delay my success,' he murmured. 'You're trying to distract me—'

'Because you're cheating.'

'No, I'm not.' He smiled a little bitterly and released her. 'I think that's your speciality.'

'The clues,' she gritted as he stepped back. 'You're getting them too quickly. Did you search a spoiler page online? I change up the clues frequently to counteract them.'

'I didn't look them up, you're watching my raw talent.' He focused on figuring out the final task.

'When I'm determined to achieve something, I
don't let anything get in the way of my goal. Like
you.'

'You know what you want and you go for it.'

'As do you.'

She wasn't his equal—but she could pretend.
Because she wanted to be. She really wanted to
be. If she could hold her own with Ramon Fernandez, she could hold her own with anyone.

'You use numerical patterns. Ciphers. The envelope contained a decoder,' he said. 'A colour
wheel. Morse code.'

'We use many codes, trick props. But sometimes it's simply that the truth is the opposite of
how it appears.'

She watched as he worked through the penultimate clue with annoying ease.

'The opposite.' He glanced across and read her
expression. 'The door will unlock if I do this?'
He smiled but didn't move the piece into play.
'Less than an hour. Time to keep your end of the
bargain.'

There was so much that was more important
than testing him like this. 'Are my parents really
going to lose their hotel?'

'It's in trouble. Your ex-husband didn't do such
a great job as assistant manager. You left and he
stayed.'

Right. So now Ramon knew that her father had
sided with her ex after she'd walked out. Callum

had remained as assistant manager while both he and her father had tried to convince her to come back. Well, Callum had tried to convince her with increasingly startling desperation while her father had simply bullied and threatened. Neither liked not having complete control.

'He left once he agreed to the divorce,' she said. Once she'd publicly humiliated him too much.

'Your father hasn't made wise choices since.'

'He tends not to make wise choices.'

He thought he did. He thought he knew everything and wouldn't listen to alternative ideas. The only way was *his* way.

She watched Ramon step closer to her. 'Dad's financial issues don't make marrying off Ashleigh the right thing to do.'

Ashleigh shouldn't be driven out of the only home she'd known. Shouldn't be expunged from the family like Elodie had been.

'Don't worry, *that* wedding will not happen.'

But Ramon wanted another one. Her heart thudded.

He frowned. 'You still look worried.'

'Of course I'm worried.'

'Don't be. I'm a good guy, helping save your sister.'

'By taking advantage of—'

'*No one* takes advantage of you, Elodie Wallace. You'll get what you want as much as I will from this.'

She stared at him. What she really wanted was *selfish*.

'Say yes and you'll have more than you need to help your sister,' he said. 'You'll have your own business. You'll be able to secure Bethan's job too. I understand she also walked out on her marriage.'

'That's right.' She tilted her chin in defiance of all his damned invasive research. 'We have our own divorced wives club, actually.'

'Of course you do. Does it have a name?'

'You mean your team didn't find that out for you? FFS.'

'Quite.'

'No, that's the *name*.'

'Standing for the obvious.'

'We're the Forever Free Sisters. Meaning we're going to be free—from *marriage*—forever. None of us are making that mistake again.'

'And with me you won't be,' he said. 'You're an astute woman, why not get what you can from me?'

'My body is not for sale.'

'Sure, but your signature could be. That's all I'm paying for. Your signature on a wedding certificate.'

She swallowed. It was a little more than that. It was her name. Her honour. But she'd destroyed both of those things herself, hadn't she?

'We both have pasts. We both know what we're getting into. We both know our affair is as inevitable as our next breath,' he said harshly. 'So why not extract some additional benefit to our being together?'

He thought she was something she wasn't, but if he knew the truth of her first marriage, if he knew how she'd faked most of those photos, how inexperienced she actually was—especially compared to him—would he still suggest this?

Elodie swallowed. He was more powerful. More experienced. More everything. If she told him and if he still wanted to proceed with this crazy plan, then she would lose what little power she had. So he couldn't know.

Because she'd spent most of last night regretting that she'd stopped him touching her.

Her loss of control had been shocking. Yet because of that she now knew he wouldn't demand more than she was willing to give. Not physically. She'd inadvertently tested him in the course of her own confusion and overwhelm. He'd stopped the instant she'd asked him to. He would again. So maybe she could fake her way through this. He never need know the extent of her inexperience and along with securing Ashleigh's future, she would get something *she* wanted. Him. Just for a little while.

'Come on, Elodie.' He crowded her as he had last night. As if he couldn't stand to stay at a respectable distance from her for more than three seconds. 'You know it's going to happen.'

'Are you trying to seduce me into saying yes?'

'As if you've never seduced someone into doing something you want?' He laughed.

Right. Elodie *had* never seduced anyone. She'd flirted—but only so far—then she was very good at escaping. And she didn't get seduced. She didn't lose herself in desire and heat. Never had. But she *wanted* to know. She *wanted* to be normal. This was her secret reason to say yes. But it had to stay a secret.

The physical relationship between them was to be a separate issue. She had an opportunity to discover something for herself. And right now it was the only thing she could think about.

'You know how this game works,' he murmured. 'The stakes aren't even that high. Neither of us is going to get hurt.'

Right. What was another failed marriage to her name? Maybe hardly anyone needed to even know about it. Surely it would be brief. Just long enough to secure a safe future for her sister and ensure he had the assets he wanted.

'You're too smart to turn down a deal that benefits you and those you care about so greatly. You're a realist, Elodie. You know what you want and you know you can get it all from me.'

Affair. Benefits. No complication. No messy misunderstandings. No expectations that couldn't be met. She'd sworn not to get hurt by a man again. And she wouldn't, because this was simply an arrangement. There was nothing deeper—no emotional connection. No guilt. But he could give her something she'd never had.

He watched her hesitation with raised brows. 'It's not like you consider wedding vows to really mean anything, right?'

That hurt but at the same time helped narrow her focus. He wanted her but didn't think much of her. She could hate him a little for that. Which was good. It would protect her from his immense magnetism.

'It doesn't bother me that you broke them before,' he added. 'They mean little to me either.'

She didn't believe him. He *judged*.

'So this is to be an open marriage?' she questioned even as the idea repelled her.

'Oh, *no*.'

His immediate guttural denial made her skin prickle and he captured her in a hard embrace.

'My affairs are always monogamous.' He lifted her chin so she couldn't avoid his eyes. 'I won't cheat on you.'

The strangest sensation of trust washed over her—belief in him—a fragile thing that scared her into pushing back. Because she couldn't drown in it. She'd believed someone once before when he'd made promises.

'I don't care if you do,' she lied, purely to keep him distanced.

'To be clear,' he said harshly, 'you won't cheat

on me either.' He ran his hand firmly down her back, moulding her against his rock-hard frame. 'You won't have the time or the energy to even consider it. I intend to keep you utterly exhausted.'

His heat and strength seeped into her. This was a threat she knew he'd honour. And just like that he got her. Her overwhelming physical response was unlike anything in her life.

'Wow,' she breathed to mask her trembling. 'Big promises.'

'Big enough to satisfy you.' His smile was more a baring of teeth. 'Say yes already.'

This was what she wanted. Him roused. Her on fire. To the point where thinking was impossible. There was only feeling. It compelled her to soften and lean right against him.

'Elodie?' He jerked her closer into an intimate embrace.

His hand lifted, gazing her breast. His erection dug into her lower belly. Her nipples pebbled hard against his hand. But her physical acceptance was not enough.

'Fine.'

Not the word he wanted but the meaning was the same. He grunted and smashed his mouth on hers. She moaned, bowing into him so he scooped her closer still.

The kisses destroyed her. She clawed him closer as the animal inside overtook her again so swiftly. He was so *hot* and she wanted him everywhere.

He *knew* because he moved almost as fast as she needed him to—unbuttoning her blouse to press kisses down her neck while hungrily grinding his hips against hers in that shamelessly sensual dance. Hell, they were almost consummating the deal while still fully clothed and it was *so* arousing. Elodie moaned.

Ramon wedged his hand between them, sliding it beneath her waistband until he got his fingers right between her legs and she moaned into his mouth again.

'Three steps ahead again, Elodie?' he growled.

'So?' She gasped in stunned pleasure at his repeated—deeper—incursion. 'Are you going to catch up?'

He laughed and suddenly dropped to his haunches, lifting her long skirt up and out of his way in a flagrant move. She just fell back against the wall as he shoved her panties down and exposed her core to his fierce gaze. To his mouth.

'What are you doing?' she whispered harshly. But she was so shocked she just let him. So willing she actually widened her stance and bunched her skirt in her hands to hold it high. So thrilled she couldn't catch her breath.

'I'm locked in here until I satisfy your demands, no?' he growled against her.

Utterly overwhelmed, she was unable to resist the temptation he offered. *Pleasure.*

'You're stunning,' he ground huskily, trailing his fingers over her thighs.

Never in her life had she been so bold. There was no embarrassment—*nothing* could survive this heat other than the desire that fuelled it. She craved his touch. She'd been craving it all night. And it was his fault. He'd awakened this hunger and with a singular circling motion she demanded he sate it.

To her gasping delight he teased his fingers over her and his mouth followed. There was no thinking. Only feeling. Wanting. Every stroke. Every lap of his tongue. She quaked as pleasure fired along every nerve. She wanted him to devour her and he did. Until a high-pitched moan startled her back to earth.

'Oh, *no*.' She bucked her hips to break his hold as she realised that mewling cry had come from her. She'd turned off the cameras and intercom, but the walls weren't going to be soundproof enough for the explosion coming upon her.

'Bite on this,' he ordered harshly.

She blinked at him uncomprehendingly, stunned to see that he'd risen.

'You're seconds from screaming your head off,' he added gruffly. 'Bite on this.'

Her mouth slackened and he shoved his silk handkerchief in before dropping back to his knees. She moaned in mortification but now it was muffled. Helplessly, hopelessly relieved, she closed her eyes and moaned again. His broad, strong hands squeezed her thighs, parting her for his mouth. She gripped her skirt as he took her so intimately with his tongue again. His fingers teased. Filling her just enough to be devastating. She rocked her hips, wanting more of him to ride. He gave her another. Pulsing, then plunging faster and deeper, he sucked too deliciously hard right where she was too devastatingly sensitive. He pulled her under with a relentless rhythmic onslaught that destroyed the last of her defences until she lost it entirely on a shriek of surrender. She gritted her teeth into the gag, grateful it suffocated her screams and then she was so far gone she simply didn't care any more.

Because he didn't stop, even as she arched uncontrollably and sobbed in uncontrolled, feral ecstasy, he gave her more. Holding her harder, his fingers flicking faster, his mouth hot and hungry until her legs gave out. That's when he caught her, rising to his feet and pressing her body against the wall with his. She trembled uncontrollably as he took the material from her mouth, wiped his own with it before shoving it into his pocket. She watched, stunned and turned on again by the total intimacy of that act and the even more carnal one preceding it. She'd never been this intimate. Never let go of everything. Never been as out of control. And she still wasn't herself. She still wasn't done. She felt his hardness pressing against her—where she needed him. If it weren't for the clothes in the way—

'Please...' She was barely aware as the raw plea escaped her. Barely aware of what she was asking for. She simply ached, unable to bear the agony of unfulfilled lust.

'Luscious Elodie,' he growled as he pinned her. 'So hedonistic. No wonder...' He breathed out harshly. His body was primed, pressing close enough to leave an imprint on her. 'When I finally have you, it will not be in a semipublic place with the possibility of interruption at any moment. It'll be in a bed, and we'll have all night and several days beyond to indulge in each other. There'll be no distractions. No interruptions.'

She shivered at the prospect. Impossibly all the more aroused. Because she believed him. He'd given her the most intense release of her life earlier. He'd just made her brainless.

She was utterly vulnerable. Utterly exposed. He'd turned her into a writhing, hot creature desperate for his touch. Shaken by the intensity of it all, she put her hand to her face to hide. How much she still ached. She heard him mutter something and he pulled back from the blatant thrust of possession into a looser, gentler embrace.

'You'll be my sole focus. I'll be yours. Together we'll be filthy,' he said unevenly. 'But it'll be *after* the wedding.'

With a muffled sob of laughter, she rested her

forehead on his chest and closed her eyes. Sure, she should straighten and take her own weight. Not lean on him like some weakling. But she was too wobbly. Still too *needy*. Lust still howled within her. If she was the confident woman he thought she was, she would prowl down his body now—freely purr on all fours, undo his trousers, tease him as he'd teased her. She would touch him. She would take him in her mouth. She would rub—

She clenched her fist, unthinkingly pressing it into Ramon's chest as she tried to stop the X-rated images in her head turning her on all over again. She'd never wanted to do that with anyone. Ever. She'd had sex only with her ex-husband and he'd never made her feel *that*. Never made her want to reciprocate in such—

How was she to have known? Why couldn't she have known? She squeezed her fist more tightly, *hating* her humiliating past. She'd never initiated sex. She'd invented reasons not to be intimate. She'd lied to her ex-husband. Repeatedly. But she'd been begging Ramon just now. *Begging.* Because the pleasure she'd just experienced, she wanted again.

A little thrown by the intensity of the storm he'd just incited, Ramon adjusted his footing to steady them both. He kept hold of her—she was trembling too much to stand on her own two feet. He covered her tightly held fist with his hand and tried to claw back his own calm while she rode out the emotion sweeping through her in a series of violent aftershocks.

She still wouldn't look at him. And she'd looked almost stricken in the immediate aftermath of her orgasm, she'd pressed her face into his shirt and hadn't lifted it since. Was she embarrassed? He shook his head to clear his thoughts. Not possible.

Yet last night her 'no' had emerged just as she'd been about to come apart on his dining table. At the time he'd thought she'd wanted him to stop but he'd realised she'd been muttering to *herself*. Today it had almost happened again until he'd thought to silence her self-consciousness. He'd wanted her to have the release. Wanted to taste it. Wanted it again now.

It was shocking how much he wanted it.

'Don't think you have to hide your hunger from me,' he growled. 'I am not so prehistoric to think a woman has any less right to pleasure than a man. You like sex. So do I.'

Her wordless, quivering response almost unravelled him. If they weren't in a semipublic place he'd be plunging balls-deep inside her right now. He tensed, battling the surging hunger *he* couldn't yet control. Winning her acquiescence to his— frankly mad—scheme had him wildly exhilarated. That's why he'd just lost his mind and gone down on her like some ravenous sex beast, right? He held her more tightly as another intense wave washed through them both. This was the most savage ache he'd ever experienced. She smelt good. Tasted good. Felt good. He wanted more. Now. Because she was still hungry too. As aroused as he.

It was unfathomable that he felt this rabid about getting her to bed. He'd thought he'd escaped his father's weakness. He'd always been able to walk away from a woman easily enough. But he'd do almost anything to have Elodie. And that *was* dangerous. She freely admitted being a liar and an adulteress. But the intensity of their sexual chemistry would be expunged and if he had to feel this kind of madness, at least it was with a woman who was experienced enough to know how it would end and who wouldn't be hurt.

'What you did before you met me is your business. Your past is your past,' he muttered, reminding himself of that reality more than anything.

That was when she lifted her head. 'I don't need your absolution.'

He released her and she immediately stepped away. But there was an interesting rush of colour beneath her skin as if she *were* embarrassed. Which didn't really make sense.

'No?' he questioned.

A spark of rebellion glittered in her pale face.

'You can still go dancing, anytime you like.' He suddenly wanted to make her strike again. 'I know you like dancing a lot.'

She straightened her blouse. 'You're not worried I might dance with other men?'

'If I'm not there your bodyguard will see off any threats.'

'My *what*?'

He smiled, happy to see her fire return. 'Naturally you'll have a bodyguard. More than one, at times.'

'You're not serious.'

Deadly, actually. 'I'm extremely wealthy. It would be remiss of me not to provide protection for you. I won't have you endangered because of your association with me.'

'They don't sound like bodyguards, more like gaolers.' She looked mutinous. 'I don't want you to control my actions.'

His amusement died. 'The *last* thing I want to do is control you.' In fact, the *only* person he wanted to control right now was himself. But that hunger sliced anew, and another truth emerged before he could stop it. 'I want to *enjoy* you.'

But if he were wholly honest, he ached for more than that. He wanted her surrender—her total submission to the passion that had ignited between them so unexpectedly. So irrationally. He didn't want control or her obedience, but he did want her to admit this was like *nothing* else she'd ever experienced.

Ego. In other words. The competitive nature that had pushed him to be top of class was on fire today. He mocked himself. He just wanted to be the best she'd ever had. He wanted to be the one she would never, ever forget. Because he already knew he was never, ever forgetting her. And that was infuriating.

But now she turned, pulling back completely. 'So how did you want to go about this? Are we to have a wedding in Vegas at two a.m.? Five minutes in a neon chapel?' She smoothed one of the silver coasters on the table needlessly. Turned and adjusted another glass.

Ramon watched her fidgeting and suspected she was more shaken by what had just happened than she wanted to admit. Frankly, so was he. They needed to get out of here and deal with everything properly. He needed to calm down.

'Sadly no, we're in too much of a hurry.' He reached for his jacket. 'Ashleigh's engagement is being announced this weekend. Isn't that why you hunted me down in the first place? I assume you have a current passport?'

'I thought you just said we weren't going to Vegas?'

'Not quite that far. We fly today. Get married tomorrow. Return before the engagement party. Our families are having a private celebration the night before and we're going to gatecrash it.'

At that she turned and shot him a mocking look. 'Why Ramon, you have a flair for the dramatic.'

'Well, you enjoy the dramatic.' He gestured

around the room they were in. 'You like to create a scene.'

'A pretend one. For *other* people to enjoy.'

'Isn't that exactly what we're doing?' he drawled.

She fiddled with another prop. 'I'll need a couple of moments with Bethan.'

He smiled ruefully. 'How will she cope with your defection from the single-forever divorcees' club?'

'She'll be busy looking after the escape rooms for me and Phoebe is currently abroad. I'll fudge the reality—'

'No scruples about deceiving her?'

'I've already told you I lie. I bluff in my business all the time. So rest assured, I'm good at it.'

Yeah. Ramon slowly followed her from the room. Warned, wary but utterly willing as he took one last look at the little clue stuck on the back wall of the hidden compartment she'd appeared in.

Trust No One

He really didn't need the reminder.

CHAPTER SIX

ELODIE TOUCHED HER CHEEK, regretting her rash decision to turn up the temperature in the escape room and still battling to contain her jumbling emotions. What had just happened? *How* had that just happened? How had she lost all control, so completely? And was she really just going to go off with this man?

Yes, she was. *For Ashleigh.* She muttered her sister's name like a mantra, desperate to keep her sister uppermost in her mind—not her own ravenous desire that had materialised the moment she'd set eyes on him and apparently could overrule her common sense as easily as pie.

As she approached reception, Bethan's eyes widened.

'Are you okay?' Bethan leaned across the counter and whispered. 'You're really flushed and your blouse is—' Bethan broke off only to immediately add, 'What—'

'I'm fine,' Elodie interrupted hastily. 'But I have to go away for a few days. Can you look after the rooms? Get one of the part-timers to—'

'Go where?' Bethan gaped.

'I know it's sudden.' Elodie slapped on a reassuring smile. 'I'm working on a deal to secure our future, but I just need—'

'A deal with *him*?' Bethan shot a concerned glance over her head to where Ramon was waiting by the door. 'He doesn't look like he wants to do *business* with you, he looks like he wants to—'

'It's *fine*,' Elodie assured her urgently. She didn't want to lie to her friend. She didn't want to tell her the truth either. She would evade both options. 'Can you manage? *Please*.'

Bethan hesitated. Bethan, who was still heartbroken from the whirlwind holiday romance that had culminated in a rushed mess of a marriage, and who trusted men even less than Elodie did.

'Of course, but you stay in touch, and you call me if you need me,' Bethan whispered vehemently. *'Any time.* I'm here for you.'

Elodie squeezed her friend's shoulder. 'I know.'

Five minutes later Elodie awkwardly sat in the back of a car, avoiding meeting Ramon's far-too-smug expression. She'd caught him looking at her thoughtfully once already and now she'd finally fully recovered her self-possession she was embarrassed. But she would fake otherwise.

Be smart. Sassy. Worldly-wise. Confident...

In control, in other words.

She cleared her throat. 'Where are we going?'

'To get your passport and papers. Then we'll head to the airport.'

This was moving *fast*. But that didn't surprise her, this man was used to getting things done. 'I'm not marrying you without written confirmation of our deal.'

'I've had a prenuptial contract drawn up—'

'You were that certain I would say yes?' Her temperature ticked up again.

'I like to be prepared for all eventualities. Give me your lawyer's email and I'll send over a copy right away.'

She shot him a quelling look. 'I'm capable of reviewing a contract myself.'

'You should take independent legal advice.'

'You should assume I'm capable of looking after my own interests,' she replied coolly.

'Have it your way,' he murmured softly.

'That's how I like it,' she purred back.

There was the smallest curve to his mouth as he gazed limpidly back at her.

'So where is it?' she prompted.

His eyes gleamed and his smile deepened. 'I've put it into a series of envelopes and hidden them in various places in this car. I'll offer occasional clues, though you might find each out of order and then have to puzzle them together. The page numbers might help, but who knows.'

She gaped at him for a full second before her

burgeoning amusement bubbled out. His smile became pure grin as she giggled.

'Here.' He reached into a bag at his feet and handed her a file.

She was completely grateful for the diversion. It was bad enough that he was staggeringly beautiful, but when he made her laugh like that any last resistance fled her already weak body. Paperwork would be the perfect antidote. Beside her, Ramon had pulled another file and was already reading it.

He'd moved into work mode. She could get a grip and do the same. Thankfully, she'd taken Phoebe's advice and done evening classes in business management and contracts law once she'd settled in London. She might not have made billions like Ramon, but with her wonder assistant friend's help, she had educated herself. Hopefully, once she had control of the escape rooms she would make it even more successful. She wished she could've bid for the business on her own but she didn't have the savings. And Ashleigh's call for help now meant she needed to do whatever was necessary.

She read the neatly typed pages. Several clauses caught her attention. Upon the dissolution of their marriage, the business interests of the escape rooms would be hers in entirety. In return she would relinquish any further claim to his fortune. But there were additional benefits she'd not expected.

'You're giving money to Ashleigh?' she asked.

'My family has put immense pressure on her.'

Ramon kept reading the report in front of him. 'Consider it reparation for emotional stress. This way she can choose to study or travel without having to bow to further parental pressure.'

Elodie blinked at his generosity. 'And there's a lump sum for me.'

'You can scratch that one out if you like.' He turned the page of his own document. 'It was only in case the escape room doesn't do as well as hoped once you take over, but having seen you in action today, I know you're going to kill it.'

She was stunned by his vote of confidence in her ability.

'What?' He lifted his head and gazed directly at her after a couple moments. 'You know you're good.'

Well, she hoped so but it was nice to hear someone else say it. Especially someone as successful as him. She coughed and tried to focus. 'The trust for Ashleigh is dependent on our remaining married for a minimum of six months.'

'We don't have to live together for all that time. I just want to beat the duration of your previous marriage,' he said with a softness that was actually nerve-shreddingly sharp. 'Be better than any competition. I'm a very competitive guy.'

She gritted her teeth. 'I'm astounded there's no good behaviour clause with a special reward for my doing every little thing you want.'

'But Elodie, *I'm* your reward. This you already

know.' His eyes widened in mock innocence. 'And every little thing you do will be every little thing that *you* want.'

Elodie dropped her gaze to the papers on her lap, trying to deny the fact that her damned toes were curling. Response rushed through her. She snatched together some sarcasm. 'If it's to be so mind-blowing, what tears us apart? How am I to destroy you?'

'We'll work that out later.' He shrugged. 'It doesn't need to be anything dramatic. Neither of us will oppose the divorce. It'll be quick, easy, painless.'

Unlike her last. She breathed out slowly. This offer was too good to turn down. Too easy. He was right. She would get *everything* she wanted. 'You have a pen for me to sign?'

'Do it on the plane, Piotr will witness.' He nodded his head towards the window. 'Passport, papers—birth certificate, wedding, divorce. Make it snappy.'

She hadn't realised they'd pulled up at her tenement block. 'I don't need anything else?' she asked, irritated by his high-speed insistence. 'Toothbrush? Clothes?'

'We can get all that there. You have ten minutes before Piotr drives off.'

Pointedly, she didn't move a muscle because she was *not* jumping to his every little command. 'Are you sure you don't want to handcuff me to you and come inside with me?'

He stared at her, motionless. She stared back—words forgotten, intention to tease evaporated. Because this was no joke. Heat unfurled deep within and a dragging sensation in the pit of her pelvis pulled her inexorably towards him. *Everything* tightened. Just as she made to escape he leaned over her. Stopping her simply by narrowing his proximity.

'I've already promised I'll indulge any and all of your kinky urges once we're *married*,' he reprimanded softly.

Fire scorched her cheeks. Yes, she'd thrown a gauntlet. But he'd not just accepted it, he'd trounced her with only a few words. She swallowed. No doubt he'd had many affairs while she was a complete *faker*. Little more than a novice. She'd have to work harder—*smarter*—to hold her own with him. Indulge and yet somehow maintain some self-protection. Remembering this was *merely* an affair was the way.

'Go on.' He opened her door before slowly pulling back from her. 'The sooner we get to the airport, the sooner your sister is saved,' he taunted.

She furiously exited the car and stalked into her building. She *would* hold her own with him. And she would escape unscathed. The one thing that soothed her was that *he* hadn't been able to hide the fiery expression in his eyes. He felt this attraction as keenly as she. She grabbed her passport and file of important paperwork, changed into comfy jeans and a tee and threw a few other items into a small carryall. She needed his influence to free Ashleigh. He was willing to pay for that because he needed her name on a certificate so he could retain the property he wanted. Beyond that, his interest was only in her body. She had no real interest in *him* either—just *his* body. So she would have it. She was in control of this every bit as much as he was.

She would see Ashleigh safe. She would get her business. And she would have the first full-blooded affair of her life.

Ramon stared fixedly at the paperwork he'd been ignoring on his knee and willed time to move just a little faster. He did not want to see her home. Not her bedroom. He was *not* curious. And the last thing he wanted to think about was the other men she'd taken there. He'd never thought he'd ever be a jealous lover, but here he was—hating the thought of her kissing someone else. Of her letting someone else inside her home, her life, her body. He dragged in a deep breath, trying to quell the ferociousness of these utterly foreign thoughts overtaking his mind. He didn't think about any women like this. But Elodie Wallace was gorgeous and wilful, smart and infuriating and he could not *believe* that he'd lost all control of himself and gone at her in her *workplace*. He hadn't been able to resist. Which was not great.

Only what had happened had been so freaking *fantastic* that just the flicker of memory made him hot all over again. Aching—*battling*—he grabbed his tablet and forced his focus on making notes for his assistants. Taking time away from work was extremely out of character for him. He needed to give them extensive notes.

She lied. She cheated. Abandoned responsibility.

He repeated her self-confessed litany of moral crimes. Reminding himself to remain wary. Distanced. Yes, their chemistry was spectacular, but lust would be sated. He wouldn't allow her to cause any damage. To his curling pleasure she was back within the ten minutes he'd assigned but he said nothing, and he even managed not to reach out and touch her despite the harrowing urge he had to. He ground through more briefings for his assistants and was ridiculously relieved when they finally made it to the airstrip.

'Where are we flying to?' she asked once he'd slid his tablet into his bag.

'Gibraltar.'

'Is that a private jet?' Her eyebrows lifted as she looked at the small insignia on the plane. 'Don't tell me that's your family crest.'

'Okay then.' He pursed his lips, mock pouting to remain silent.

'You don't seriously have a family crest?' She stopped ahead of the stairs and studied it more closely. 'Of course it would feature a bird of prey,' she muttered. 'But it should be *all* the apex predators in a pile fighting with each other.'

He laughed. 'That's exactly what my family is like. I'll have it amended.'

'Along with that stupid trust for your property,' she said and marched up into the plane.

'Right.' He ushered her to a seat near a small table. 'After we take off, sign the prenup. There are more forms. Some are in Spanish.'

'I don't speak Spanish.'

'Piotr will translate.'

'Can I trust him?'

'For now you have little choice. But you're quick…you'll pick Spanish up in no time,' he said soothingly.

She shot him a mutinous look. 'Are you going to teach me?'

'As if you'd allow that,' he chuckled. 'You're more likely to download an app and teach yourself.'

She didn't respond, which meant he was right. He couldn't help smiling at her determined self-sufficiency.

'Piotr will witness then get the documents ready to file.' He handed her a pen.

'Is there nothing the man can't do?' she murmured. 'Will he be flying the plane too?'

'Don't get any ideas.' Ramon felt that jealousy ripple again and tried to lighten his response.

'He has a wife and two children. And if that isn't enough to deter you from trying to seduce him, you're not his type.' He smiled. 'You're too provocative. He likes them demure.'

But Elodie's sarcastic facade had fallen away and she looked genuinely concerned. 'Does he ever get to see them?'

Ramon's defensiveness surged. 'My bodyguards are on a week-on, week-off schedule. This is his week on.'

He took a seat on the diagonal from hers. Once they'd levelled out Piotr appeared from the rear cabin along with an assistant who offered Elodie refreshment. Ramon opened up his laptop and feigned focus while she worked on the forms but he saw she did indeed scratch out the cash provision for her. He counted down the minutes until Piotr took the documents Elodie had filled in and went back to the rear cabin.

'Are you always this work-driven?' Elodie sipped from the tall glass of juice.

'You do realise how many people my companies employ?' he gritted. Because the fact was he'd basically got nothing done, and while he could always focus on work, right now was the one exception.

'Companies?' A furrow appeared between her brows. 'Don't you mean hotels?'

'The hotels come under one company. There are several *other* companies.' He stared at her.

'Didn't you do any research on me?' Was he actually miffed by that?

'Obviously not enough seeing I didn't know you have a cousin with almost the exact same name as you. But then we can't all afford an army of assistants with the skills to hack into people's private databases.'

'Your social media profiles were all set to *public*.'

'What other companies?' she redirected pointedly.

'The luxury leather goods. The vineyards. There's a venture into a cruise line.' He slowly listed them off, rather enjoying her mounting outrage. 'Then there's the other properties.'

'You're CEO of all of them? How is that even possible? You can't oversee the work of absolutely everyone.'

'You'd be surprised how much detail I can retain on each,' he said. 'I like the variety. I need that challenge.'

Her mouth opened. Then closed. Then she sat back. For a second she'd almost looked crestfallen, which diverted him momentarily. Why would his work commitments disappoint her?

'What do you want me to wear to the wedding?' she muttered after another few minutes.

For the first time in years Ramon's brain froze. 'You can buy a dress once we get to Gibraltar,' he said stiffly.

'Ooh, are you going to give me a platinum card so I can drain all your massive accounts?'

He breathed out through clenched teeth. 'Haven't had time for that paperwork yet, darling. So sorry. Piotr will pay.'

'You mean he's going to keep me on a leash.'

Awfully, another ripple of jealousy ripped through him. He tensed—too busy battling it to answer her immediately.

'You don't have *any* requests?' she prodded, unaware of how close to the edge he was. 'Do you want something outrageous or would you prefer traditional?'

Have mercy. He closed his eyes—couldn't stand to think of her in a wedding gown—*any* gown—in this instant. She'd look stunning in anything and best of all *naked*. And he was losing his mind. He hauled his papers together and stood, inwardly swearing because they were airborne and he *desperately* needed some space.

'You can wear whatever you like,' he snapped. 'I need to work.'

Elodie stared as he strode towards the back of the plane. Okay, so he really didn't care what she wore, which she should be pleased about. She'd had her clothing choices dictated to her for most of her life—no pink, no red, no short hemlines…

Yet absurdly she had the urge to make Ramon *pay* for his disinterest. There was literally, of course. She could spend squillions on some outrageous frock, which would serve him right, it really would. Maybe he thought she'd be restrained with Piotr in tow? Or maybe she'd turn up in a bin bag. He probably wouldn't notice if she did and she'd feel rubbish. She didn't want to feel rubbish, she wanted to feel good—wanted a dress that *she* liked. Maybe she'd go shopping and pick something solely for *herself.* After all, she'd not chosen her own wedding dress in her marriage to Callum. She'd had to wear the 'fairy tale' number her father had approved of. 'Modest' and 'appropriate', it had been lacy and swamped her. She didn't want to be modest or appropriate this time.

This was definitely not a fairy tale.

Her marrying Ramon was going to be scandalous. But she didn't care about the optics. She wanted to feel *sexy.* And she didn't want to examine her motivations for that.

She ruminated for an hour, absurdly irritated by Ramon's ability to focus on work while she was being driven to distraction at the thought of their marriage. As for all the companies he managed… His need for *challenge* and *variety*… That told her their marriage was likely lasting way *less* than six months. He'd probably be bored and ready for his next female 'challenge' in days. Sure, he'd said his affairs were monogamous but that didn't mean they lasted long. Had he had a succession of lovers before her? She didn't even know, yet here she was. Jealous.

Grumpily determined to course-correct, she opened her phone and took advantage of the on-board Wi-Fi to download a language app. Ten minutes of basic greetings later, she needed a bathroom break and headed towards the back of the plane.

That's when she heard a weird noise. She peeked through the gap in the door leading to the rear cabin. 'Oh, for...' She gritted back the rest of her mutter.

Ramon paused dictating voice messages and grinned at her. 'Something to say?'

He'd shed his stunning suit and was now clad in gym shorts and singlet, apparently sweating out his aggravations, and looked even more gorgeous while he *still* worked.

'I cannot believe you have an indoor cycle on an airplane,' she said stonily. The machine was bolted to the floor.

'It helps with jet lag.'

He was so *perfect*, wasn't he? So controlled. Physically active, he ate well, and worst of all, he was still reading a report while doing it. Multi-tasking with his annoying ability to concentrate.

'You really are a workaholic,' she muttered.

'You will be too once you get back.' He smiled at her patronisingly. 'Your business will be everything.'

'It wasn't a compliment.' She corrected him. 'Is money all that matters to you?'

'It's not money that drives me but the company itself. It's my heritage and my responsibility and I'm proud that I've grown it.'

'It's your baby.'

'As the escape room is yours.' He scooped up the towel on his handlebar and wiped his brow. 'Admit it. You work hard to make it thrive.'

'Yes. But unlike you I also have other things in my life.'

'Because your baby is somewhat smaller than mine. Mine is demanding.'

'You could delegate.'

'Why? What am I missing?'

'Rest and relaxation?' she quipped lightly, barely masking her deep curiosity. 'A social life?'

'Like you have? Dancing with all your men?'

'Dancing with my *friends*,' she replied nonchalantly. 'If men want to dance with us, that's fine too. It's a more fun option than *your* stress release. *Cycling*.'

He stopped pedalling. 'Well, tomorrow night I'll be riding you and I think you'll be grateful I burned some energy here already.'

She gaped at him. 'You're appalling.'

'Because you make it so worthwhile.' He hopped off the bike and moved towards her. 'For a party girl with no conscience and no cares, you blush amazingly easily.'

She locked her weak knees so she wouldn't back away from him. 'I'm not blushing. This is my natural colouring. Red.'

'Rot.' He placed the backs of his fingers against her cheek. 'You're burning up.'

'Fever.'

'Yeah, commonly known as lust.' He laughed. 'As stunning as I know we're going to be together, we're definitely waiting until our wedding night so *stop* trying to tempt me.'

She wanted to tell him he'd be waiting a long time but couldn't lie that well.

'It's my first, you know?' Sardonic amusement danced in his eyes. 'Marriage, that is. Special.'

'Are you going to wear white?' she gritted acerbically.

'I can't tell you that!' he declared with mock outrage. 'It's bad luck to see each other in our wedding finery before the ceremony.'

'Bad luck is the least of your concerns.' She turned and stomped back to the forward cabin.

She desperately tried not to stare at him when he returned to the seat beside hers a half hour later. He'd seemingly *showered* onboard and was now dressed in a different suit, smelt delicious and looked more vital and virile than ever. And she was not thinking about the bed she'd seen in that cabin at the back of the plane.

Once they'd landed, Ramon guided Elodie into the waiting car. They went straight from the airport to a civic office where they registered their intention to marry. In twenty-four hours they could proceed. Then they went to the hotel—which would also be their wedding venue. Oceanfront and opulent, their suite had the most stunning views of the sea.

'I have work to do.' Ramon set his bag by the large desk in the lounge.

So predictable.

'Good stuff,' Elodie said airily. 'You need to earn many more millions because I'm taking Piotr shopping for the outrageously expensive dress that you don't care about.'

'Did that wound?' He smiled at her dangerously. 'Don't worry darling, I care very much about what's *beneath* it.'

Elodie had to get out of there before she devolved and did something physical to him—and not in a good way.

'We need to find an evening wear specialist, Piotr. Are you up to it?' she asked the enigmatic bodyguard.

'I have a list of boutiques and phoned ahead to make several private appointments,' he answered. 'There's also a hairdresser and beautician at the hotel on standby should you like to make use of them later.'

Good grief, the man was worth his well-muscled weight in gold. 'I hope Ramon pays you ridiculously well,' she said. 'I don't know how you put up with his round-the-clock demands.'

'He's a good employer. He doesn't demand all that much.'

'He's listening in right now, isn't he? In your earpiece. And you've just earned yourself a bonus.'

'This trip is a bonus. It is the first time in three years I've known him to travel for leisure.'

Elodie paused, startled by the nugget of information she'd never have expected the utterly discreet Piotr to let fall. But this trip *wasn't* leisure. It was business. And all work and no play made Ramon Fernandez a formidable opponent.

Ninety minutes and three shops later, Elodie stood in the private changing room and stared at her reflection. The shop assistants would admire her in anything—which meant she was reliant on her own judgement. She had to please no one but *herself.* She liked her costumes at work—pretending, being in character. But this was something just for *her.*

The soft silk skimmed her body, sophisticated, sexy, sweet too. It might not please him—it might not be the bold statement he expected from her—but *she* loved it.

Energised and excited, she decided to find something equally confidence boosting to wear to the family cocktail party they were going to gatecrash to stop Ashleigh's engagement. Oh, yes, Elodie Wallace was finally on her game.

CHAPTER SEVEN

RAMON HAD MOUNTAINS of work to do, and he was not going to let a little thing like getting married disrupt his routine. He absolutely was not bothered that Elodie had been gone for more than three hours already. Yet he'd lost track of the number of times he'd gone to the suite's media room to glance out the window overlooking the hotel entrance and now here he was wandering over to do it again. His concentration was blown and pushing him into feral territory. Which was *not* him. He did not abandon all responsibility just because he wanted *sex*. He was not his father.

Only this time as he looked out the window, he spotted her walking into the hotel. His entire body responded with a savage driving urge that almost overwhelmed him. He breathed deep and glanced wide, amused to see Piotr, masking a pained expression as he walked a step behind her, laden with bags. Was she making a stand with her purchases?

He sure as hell hoped so. He couldn't wait to see the contents of them. He couldn't wait to touch her.

It wasn't for the wedding that he was really holding off. It was to test his own self-control. He was determined that he wasn't a lecherous, rampantly reckless man like his father. Turns out he was exactly that. And to make it worse, he was now so tightly wound he no longer cared about the fact.

The second she appeared in the hotel suite he moved towards her. 'You must be exhausted.'

She might want to lie down—in which case he would join her. He utterly abandoned the idea of keeping his hands off her until after the wedding. The ceremony would happen regardless and was honestly irrelevant. He could and would have her. Now.

'Not at all.' Elodie evaded his approach with a swift step and a coolly proud gaze. 'I have an appointment with a hairdresser and a beautician. Possibly a make-up artist.'

He stilled, locking in place in the middle of the lounge. Every muscle burned with the urge to touch her—to provoke her the way she provoked him by merely *existing*—let alone with the levelling look that accompanied her words.

'You should cut your hair,' he muttered huskily. 'Tie it up at least.'

She froze and that levelling look of hers iced.

Ramon tried but couldn't suppress his smile because he was sure she would do the opposite. She blinked a couple times and her mouth softened. He remained rock-still as she walked over until she stood right in front of him. Which yes, was another thing he'd desperately wanted. She rose on tiptoe, bringing her lips dangerously close to his ear. He went from rock-still to diamond-hard.

'Is that your juvenile way of saying you like my hair long and loose?' she murmured.

Of course she had him. '*You're* the one who likes things to mean the opposite of what's true.'

Her eyes gleamed. 'I'll do my hair how I want.'

'Great,' he croaked in total capitulation. 'Can't wait.'

Because he'd weave his hands into her hair *however* she styled it—he was desperate to feel its silky length and wrap himself in her fire. Pleasure flashed in her eyes as with a tilt of her chin she shot him the smallest smile. Helplessly he watched her leave with a sway to her hips utterly designed to aggravate and arouse him even more.

He couldn't stand to remain cooped up inside while she was out. He left the hotel, turned down a couple of streets, vaguely taking in the shop fronts. He didn't shop in person. His assistants ensured the clothes he needed were in ready supply, knowing his preferred brands. His tailor made house calls for fittings. He never had need to purchase anything personal.

But one sign caught his eye, the window pulled him closer, and a quixotic impulse pushed him inside. He couldn't recall being in a jewellery store. Had never bought anything for himself or anyone else. Such gestures were meaningless—his father had showered his mother with sparkling gifts and flowery attentions to hide his infidelity. She'd believed him, accepted them. Ramon had refused to treat dates with trinkets. But this deal with Elodie was different. It was a tease. He would get something to provoke her. Only then one item caught his eye and it wasn't a provocation.

It was perfect.

Almost two hours later he stood by the window overlooking the sea and considered making the leap. He needed to cool off somehow. He'd been dressed and waiting for her to appear from her room for more than fifteen minutes. No one kept him waiting. Ever. Yet here he was, almost bursting out of his skin from the agony and irritation of waiting. He finally heard the door open and spun.

'Oh, were you waiting? So sorry.' Her voice was breathy as she sauntered towards him, head high, eyes glinting.

Once again Ramon couldn't stop the smile spreading across his face. 'You really do like playing games.'

She was pure party girl in a backless, short, scarlet, sexy as hell, form-fitting dress. Her hair was left long and loose and the urge to run his hands through it was going to destroy him.

'I'm not the only game-player here.' Her gaze swept down his sleek tuxedo.

'You suit red,' he muttered.

'My father said I should never wear it.'

'Is that why you wore little else for a while?' He moved closer as her eyes flashed. 'In all those pictures in those clubs,' he said, explaining how he'd seen them. 'You don't like being told what you can and cannot do.'

'Maybe I got a little sick of it,' she said quietly.

'If he dictated what you were allowed to wear then I don't blame you for rebelling.'

She turned her head slightly away from him.

'It was more than what you could wear, huh?' Her father really was the controlling type.

She nodded and glanced back. 'I think I'll be overly reactive now when people try to issue instructions.'

'No, you?' He'd chuckle if he weren't so strung out. 'So, are you wearing red for our wedding?'

Her lashes fluttered, suddenly coy. 'I thought we were keeping such details secret.'

Anticipation pulled every muscle tight. But she backed away, held up her phone and snapped a selfie with the view of the ocean in the background.

'You're updating your social media profile?' he mocked.

'Sending a proof-of-life picture to my friends,' she replied primly. 'I go silent for more than twenty-four hours and there'll be an international incident.'

'They'll launch a divorced wives rescue mission?'

'Exactly.'

'You don't want me in the picture?' He prowled closer.

'And give up our element of surprise?' She shook her head. 'No *way*.'

Right. He stilled—he was the one surprised. He'd got so caught up in baiting her he'd forgotten the reason *why* they were getting married at all.

Elodie wasn't hungry enough to do the divine dinner justice. She didn't need the fuel—she was running on something else—something she couldn't quite handle.

'I have something for you.' He put a small square box on the table once the waiting staff had removed their plates.

She wasn't just out of her depth and struggling to stay afloat. She was sunk in concrete.

'Aren't you going to open it?'

'Not if it's what I think it is.'

'We're getting married, Elodie. You do need the trimmings.'

'*Trimmings?* Am I some celebratory dinner to be served up on a table?'

His grin was wolfish and she snatched up the box in annoyance at her own ability to make appalling *double-entendres*.

'Don't panic,' he said a few moments later as she stared at the ring in stunned silence. 'It's artificially grown in a lab. Machine-made. Not worth anywhere as much as you're thinking.'

'So it's as fake as this marriage is going to be?' She tried to match his droll tone. 'All that glitters is most definitely not gold.'

'Such a pity, isn't it?' he muttered wickedly.

Elodie had seen a fair amount of costume jewellery because they used it in the escape rooms all the time and Bethan could turn pound shop items into trinkets that looked like they were worth millions. But this *looked* an absolute treasure—full throttle dramatic. So she had the feeling this ruby wasn't lab grown and nor were the diamonds surrounding it. She lifted her gaze, all faux insouciance. 'Yes. It's disappointing that it won't be worth much when I sell it in a few months.'

'You won't sell it,' Ramon purred. 'You're a magpie. You like collecting shiny, worthless things—'

'To feed my shiny worthless soul?' She managed to slide the ring onto her finger despite her cold sweat, and lifted her hand to see the stones catch the light. 'Careful, you'll increase my appetite for more trinkets. I might demand actually *valuable* ones, then you'll be in trouble.'

He just laughed.

She couldn't take her eyes off the ring. It was a statement piece. Definitely unusual and one of a kind. Panic subsumed her. 'It's not a family heirloom, is it?' She looked up at him. 'Not your mother's or anything inappropriate like that?'

He actually recoiled. 'Why on earth would you think it was my *mother's*?'

'Well, when did you have the chance to buy it? When did? *Oh!*' She broke off, suddenly feeling a fool. 'Piotr has exquisite taste. Please thank him for choosing so well.'

The strangest expression crossed Ramon's face—a quixotic blend of admiration and indignation. 'You vexatious wretch.'

'Forgive me if I don't believe for a second that you took time out of your precious work schedule to choose something so unimportant.' Elodie smiled.

He drank almost the entire glass of ice-cold water in one go before sucking in a breath. 'I'm going to make you pay for that.'

'I can hardly wait.' She faked cool but her breathlessness betrayed her.

Had he chosen it? She looked at it again, still doubting his word on its artificial origins. But her clueless question made her realise she didn't know anywhere near enough about him. She had no idea where his parents were, let alone what they would think of their son marrying a complete stranger. He hadn't mentioned them at all. 'What will she think of this?'

'Who?' he frowned.

'Your mother. What's she going to think of your sudden marriage?'

He froze. Then rallied. 'Both my parents are dead. They won't think anything.'

'Sorry.' She felt terrible but at the same time it was hardly her fault—the man had more walls than a Renaissance hedge maze. 'I didn't know—'

'And you don't really need to.'

'I disagree,' she said flatly. She'd never been as argumentative with anyone in her life. 'But if we're to have everyone believe this marriage is real—for the duration—then I am going to need to, aren't I? I don't even know how old you are, let alone when your birthday is. I'll put my foot in it from the start.'

'Did you not read the marriage forms?' he replied coolly. 'I'm twenty-nine. Scorpio. My father died when I was eighteen. My mother when I was twenty-five. I'm their only child. I took over the family business when my father died and have done very little else. I live for my work.'

And he didn't want to share anything more. Okay, she got it—even if it sounded somewhat sad. 'I'm twenty-four. Also a Scorpio. That's all we need to know, right?'

To her relief his smile returned.

Elodie barely slept. Ramon had kept his distance completely after dinner. He'd quietly accompanied her back to the suite and immediately disappeared into his own room. Probably to do more work. She'd been absurdly disappointed. She'd thought she'd read hunger for *her* in his eyes before dinner but he'd backed off completely. Was this not going to be an affair—if he was that hot for her, why the delay?

Early the next morning she got out of bed and drew back the curtains. It was a stunning day and there were too many hours to fill before the ceremony. She had to move. In the lounge Ramon was nowhere to be seen. He was probably unnecessarily observing those wedding traditions—ridiculous given this wasn't a *real* wedding.

She went back to her bedroom and dressed in jeans and tee. When she went back out into the lounge she found Piotr waiting. His prescience was uncanny.

'I'd like to go for a walk, is that allowed?'

'I will accompany you discreetly.'

She rolled her eyes. 'You don't need to walk three feet behind.'

But Piotr obviously had his orders as she ambled through the town. Around her people were going about their business, tourists were taking photos, students in groups, office workers hurried to grab coffees—it was all so normal. What she and Ramon were doing really was ridiculous—who got married mid-afternoon on a *Thursday*?

She wandered along the shady side of a street she'd not ventured down yesterday in the great dress hunt, and paused by a jewellery store. She couldn't resist entering—drawn to a large glass case on the rear wall. Just the one piece was displayed. She put her hand to her chest as she stared at it. Four strands of what looked like diamonds sat flat on the back of the neck, while at the front they were woven into an intricate diamond knot—further embellished with yet more gleaming stones. If they actually *were* diamonds this one necklace would probably cost about the same as a large-sized house. Sure enough, there was no obvious price tag—which meant it would be astronomical and there was no way she could ever wear anything like it.

'You like this necklace, *señora*?'

Startled, Elodie turned as the jeweller approached. She saw his sweeping glance take her in—lingering on the fingers she'd spread just below her collarbones. He'd seen the ruby ring. She dropped her hand. No doubt the man would instantly recognise it as 'artificial'. Sure enough, his demeanour subtly changed. But to her surprise he went from merely polite, to pure sycophant.

'Would you like to try it on?' He opened the cabinet and lifted out the glittering piece before she could say no.

'Just…briefly,' she agreed weakly.

Moments later she gazed at her reflection, her resolve weakening. Maybe she would amp up her gold-digger facade? Only it wasn't that. Honestly? She loved the cool weight and drama of it. She'd never thought she'd go for something so intense or so couture but it would contrast beautifully with the light simplicity of the dress she'd chosen. But there was no way she would spend that amount of Ramon's money.

The jeweller regarded her speculatively. 'It is sublime on you.'

'Yes, but I can't...' She made the man remove the necklace.

Piotr materialised beside her. 'Do you need assistance, Ms Wallace?'

'I don't think so.' She smiled at him ruefully. 'I could never buy it.'

Piotr studied her impassively. 'What if you could borrow it? With your permission I will inquire.'

'Um—'

Piotr turned and addressed the jeweller in staccato bursts of rapid Spanish that she didn't understand a word of. After some time he turned back to her. 'I will supply a borrow bond and return it immediately after the ceremony. We'll take it with us now.'

'Really?' She was stunned.

The jeweller put the necklace into a velvet-lined travel case that Piotr slid into his jacket pocket in return for a swipe of one of those cards.

Five minutes later she couldn't resist a quiet plea to the taciturn bodyguard. 'We don't have to tell Ramon we've borrowed it, do we?'

She wanted to let her temporary husband think she'd spent a stupid amount of his money—just a tiny tease. She swore she almost caught a smile from Piotr.

'My instructions are to assist you any way necessary, Ms Wallace. You can trust that I will take care of your best interests.'

She did trust him, actually. He was a marvel.

Back at the hotel the hairdresser and make-up artist were waiting. Two hours later she stared at her reflection. A veil the hairdresser had produced added a touch more 'bridal', the necklace delivered a wallop of luxury, while the sky-high heels would give her a chance to look Ramon directly in the eyes.

But really all this was for *her*. Last time it had been everything someone else wanted. But this was all for herself and she was going to indulge in the fantasy of it because it sure as hell was never, *ever* happening again.

Piotr arrived and actually smiled as he offered her his arm like the big brother she'd never had.

The hotel had a stunning private deck that was built right over the stunning blue sea. Enormous white sails screened them from the sun overhead and Elodie breathed in deeply as she walked towards her groom. On her first wedding day she'd been anxious and awkward and scared of screwing up. This was vastly different. It wasn't meant to be momentous—she could relax—but the flutters in her belly begged to differ.

Ramon was waiting for her beneath a fresh floral

arch and was indeed wearing white. His linen suit, perfect for the blazing mid-afternoon heat, accentuated his tanned skin and the vivid blue of his eyes. Excitement trammelled through her at the sight of him. She desperately, *dangerously*, wanted him.

This was simply a *deal*. There shouldn't be any emotion, hell, he mightn't even particularly like her and she didn't want to let herself think that he *could* because it would tempt her to like him back. He was far too easy to like already. Yet suddenly it was impossible not to smile.

Ramon couldn't speak. She looked immaculate. This was simply another of her costumes except he couldn't quite believe it. With a helpless shrug he fell into the fantasy. Her dress had the thinnest of straps and skimmed her slim figure— the pale pink accentuated her stunning hair and was so very pretty. The veil was short and didn't cover her face, which he appreciated because her eyes were shining. She looked so damned fresh and *sincere*. He saw her shaky breath as she took her place beside him. She was either a supremely talented actress or she really was nervous. He reached out and took her hand. Tightened his grip when he felt her tremble. They were in this together. Just for a little while.

He repeated the promises, deeply satisfied as she echoed them, laughed when she struggled to put the wedding band on him.

'I wasn't prepared,' she muttered as the celebrant turned to deal with the paperwork. 'I didn't realise you'd wear one.'

'It's a symbol of my taken status,' he said, and winked.

'You could just adjust your social media settings. It would've been cheaper.'

'But money is no object.' His attention lingered on the diamond collar she wore around her neck. The irony of it being rope-like wasn't lost on him.

She flushed almost self-consciously and touched the knot at the base of her throat. 'I thought I'd better up the sparkle, like the greedy little magpie I am.'

'The ruby ring was not enough for you?' he murmured.

'I need to look sufficiently worthy for you. Plus, I can sell them both later and make bank.'

'Enterprising.' Ramon decided then and there that he would have her naked in his bed wearing nothing but that collar tonight. It would satisfy him immensely. And yes, he might even have to tie her there. This was only a short-term pretence so he would indulge in it while he could.

Before the celebrant could say the words he kissed her. She melted right against him but it wasn't *nearly* enough.

He'd bring forward the flight plan. He quietly moved to speak with Piotr, listened as his man explained a few salient points. Smiled. After giving

Piotr a couple extra instructions he moved back to Elodie and used the photographer as pretext to pull her close again. He couldn't resist stealing another kiss. Then he gripped her hand tightly in his and walked her out of the hotel to the waiting car.

'Where are we going?' She looked more nervous now than she had just before the ceremony. 'Somewhere for more photos?'

'No.' He quelled his amusement. 'We're going to the airport.'

'The airport? Now?' Her voice went pitchy. 'We're not staying in Gibraltar?'

'You're disappointed?' He leaned closer, curious to see how she'd play this.

'I haven't even been to the beach.'

'I'll take you to another beach sometime. One that's more private. Indulge your craving for a naked roll in the waves there.'

Her mouth opened. Closed. She took a breath. 'We're not even stopping to get changed?'

'The flight isn't that long.'

'But—'

'We need to get back to break up your sister's engagement, remember?' he said smoothly. 'There's no time to lose.'

Her tension mounted. He almost felt sorry for her, except she'd teased him one time too many today—just by existing—and he *really* wanted to call her bluff.

'We can't leave yet.' She glanced around as they

arrived at the airport. 'I need Piotr to run an errand.'

'He's busy tending to *my* errands. He'll meet us here shortly.'

'Well, *I* need to run one.'

'Can't it wait until we get back to London?' He guided her towards the plane. 'Come on, we need to get moving.'

'We can't.' She stopped dead on the tarmac and gripped his arm desperately. 'I'll get arrested.'

He stared down at her, feigning confusion. 'What? Why?'

'Because it's on loan.' She paled.

'Sorry?'

'The necklace. I can't leave Gibraltar wearing it. I promised to have it returned the moment the ceremony was over.'

Ramon couldn't hold back his amusement a second longer. 'You mean you didn't buy it?'

'Of course not!' she snapped. 'I would *never* spend so much on anything. Not my money. And definitely not *yours*!'

He stared down at her, his smile fading as he absorbed her genuine agitation—not so much from the fear of taking the diamonds from the country but that he would really think she would spend so much of his money. And she hadn't spent any at all, had she? Piotr had informed him that Elodie had very determinedly paid for her dress, shoes and accessories all herself.

'Well, I did,' he muttered roughly.

'What?' She breathed hectically.

'I bought it,' he growled. 'It suits you.'

Her eyes widened. 'Piotr said I could trust him.'

She'd been honest about the necklace and deeply concerned not to deceive the retailer. Or him. Which pleased him an odd amount. Her sweet panic compelled him to admit the truth.

'You can,' Ramon said, as he pulled her onto the plane. 'He didn't tell me it was on loan until after the ceremony. He was forced to when I asked him to get ready to leave sooner than I'd originally said. So I sent him to pay for it.'

She perched on the edge of a seat and didn't look any more relieved. 'How much did it cost?' she asked.

'I've no idea.' He slumped into the seat opposite hers.

'You don't know how much it costs?' She looked appalled.

'Apparently nor do you,' he said. 'And honestly, I don't *care* how much it costs.'

A flash of fury sharpened her eyes and her hands went to her neck.

'Keep it on,' he ordered sharply.

She froze, then lowered her hands.

Utterly goaded by her fierce glare he leaned forward. 'I'm taking you to my bed the moment we land back in London. And in that bed I will take you wearing nothing but those diamonds,

Elodie. I've been fantasising about that from the second I saw you in that dress today. Which also is delectable by the way. So don't remove a thing, because *I* want to do it.' He paused to release a stressed sigh. 'Please.'

'You're going to…' She breathed in with apparent difficulty.

'Have you. Yes. My bed. Time. Space. Privacy. So we endure the flight back. It's only three hours. Can you cope?' He was furious with both her and his descent into monosyllabic sentences.

She flushed. Her gaze fixed on him. Struggling as much as he.

They remained silent while the attendant got the flight ready and Piotr returned. Remained silent as the plane taxied down the runway and took off. And the moment they levelled out, Ramon stood to remove his jacket.

'Don't take it off,' Elodie ordered in a thin voice.

He stilled.

She lifted her chin and met his gaze squarely. 'I want to do it. Don't remove a thing.'

He sat back down. 'You like making me sweat?'

'I think it's only fair.'

Ramon stared at her. Siren. Temptress. So bloody beautiful. And finally—for now—*his*. He watched her erratic breathing, the sheen on her skin, the way she squirmed in her seat as he stared. As for the undeniable evidence of her arousal gifted to him by the sharp peaks of her luscious breasts—his body was like a rock.

'Let's play something,' he suggested tightly. Except the only games he could think of were highly inappropriate.

'You're not going to work?' she muttered.

'Currently not capable,' he conceded through gritted teeth.

Another flush of desire stained her skin. She reached into the bag the attendant had delivered and pulled out a spiral-bound notebook. 'Help me design a room I'm working on.'

He reached for a bottle of mineral water and took a moment to mentally calibrate. 'What's the theme?'

'Honeymoon suite.'

'Right.' He half laughed. 'Let me guess. Runaway bride?'

Her pout curved. 'Intriguing, don't you think? She's desperate to escape.'

'Boring. Flip it—why not a runaway groom?'

'Would he be such a coward?' She stared into his eyes.

Ramon had the feeling he should be running away right now. His want for her was insanely intense. 'Why is it okay for *her* to run away?' he pointed out tensely. 'Why wouldn't she stay and fight for her man?'

'Maybe it's not a marriage she actually wants.' She rolled her eyes. 'Who generally has the power or control in a relationship? Statistics suggest it isn't the bride. Sometimes the only way out is to escape. It's quickest, easiest. Safest.'

'Okay,' he said softly, quelling the sharp ache in his ribs that her words engendered. 'Talk me through what you have so far.'

He listened as she outlined the full 'scenario'— the few props and tricks she'd already had—then began throwing outrageous suggestions at her because he needed to lighten the mood. She swiftly matched him. They debated the merits of virtual reality and of incorporating light projections into the room.

'What if they have to evade noxious gas—you could have fun with dry ice. They'd have to put on masks. It would be fully immersive. People love wholly immersive.'

'Do they?' She laughed. 'You'll be suggesting dive tanks and flood rooms next.'

The hours literally flew by. By the time they landed, Elodie had scribbled several pages of notes while Ramon had laughed more than he had in the last decade. Which made him sober up the second he realised it.

'You're very creative, Ms Wallace,' he said softly.

She wriggled her ring-clad fingers at him. 'Not Ms anymore.'

No. She was his wilful wife, and he was damn well having his wedding night.

CHAPTER EIGHT

ELODIE STEPPED INTO the house and heard Ramon close the door behind them. The conversation that had bubbled so easily between them for hours on the flight had evaporated and she felt so awkward that even breathing seemed difficult and unnatural. Energy, adrenaline, anticipation all coursed through her, rendering her uncoordinated. But they were finally here and now it would happen. Only she didn't know how to start. Should she undress? Only he'd said he wanted to do that. Should she walk straight to his room? Only she didn't actually know which one that was. She was so skittish she stumbled on her high-heel sandals. Only he must've been right behind her because he caught her and swung her into his arms.

'Nicely done,' he murmured sardonically and tossed her lightly to pull her closer.

'You think I tripped deliberately?' She wished she *had* thought of it because she was appallingly happy to be pressed against him like this.

'I think you're very good at playing your part.' He walked swiftly down the corridor.

'Right. This isn't real,' she reminded her thudding heart with a breathless murmur.

'And yet.' He set her down on her feet. 'This is the only wedding night I'll ever have.'

'You really don't want to fall in love? Marry again later—for life?'

'No.' A smile curled his lips. 'So indulge me in the fantasy of tonight.'

'You're into role-play.'

'And you're not?' His humour flashed.

More than he would ever know. But she had no idea how to fake worldliness in this moment.

'This is so elegant.' He tracked a finger along the neckline of her silk slip dress. 'As for that diamond collar. As for *you*...'

Her heart was going to beat right out of her chest any moment. She couldn't take her gaze off him as he tangled his fingers in her hair and tilted her head back. She arched towards him. He liked her dress. Her necklace. He wanted *her*. Which was such an immense relief because he was *all* she wanted.

'Feels like I've been waiting forever for this. Going to take you apart, Elodie,' he swore. 'Going to make you come harder than you've ever come in your life.'

'Get on with it then,' she breathed. 'Enough talking.'

But she stilled as that anticipation paralysed
her. He was overwhelming and she really didn't
know where to begin. There was a curious smile
in his eyes as he studied her. Next moment he
lifted her onto the bed. A haze enveloped her as
he stood above her. She wanted to touch him but
couldn't reach, couldn't find the strength to do
anything but moan. Her fingers fluttered. Then
she couldn't do anything as he caressed her. His
fingers trailed all over her until her hips lifted
through no choice of her own. She rippled, un-
dulating on the bed, meeting his tender, teasing
strokes. So easily he made her a mindless creature
who craved anything he cared to give her—from
the lightest kisses, to the briefest of touches. When
even this—the mere play of his skilled hand—
destroyed her. He didn't even have to *kiss* her to
have her so completely his.

She was in awe as his potent sexuality over-
powered everything—until she was aroused in a
way she'd never been—wanting things she'd never
wanted and twisting restlessly until he took pity
on her and kissed her through the silk dress. It
was no less of an intimacy—of a torture.

'Ramon!' She wanted him closer.

He slid her dress up, slid her lace panties down.
His smile was feral as he watched her arch to meet
his hand and let her have just a finger. It wasn't
enough and yet she shook with need. There was

only now. Only him. In that moment he was all there would *ever* be for her.

'I can't take any more.' She trembled. 'Please, Ramon. *Please.*'

He was flushed and breathing hard, revelling in her escalation. 'What do you want?'

She shook her head, only able to gasp his name. She wanted to hold him. To feel his whole body against hers. Skin to skin. But he just teased her—devastatingly—watching her lose control at his touch.

'*Tell* me,' he groaned. A plea as much as a dare.

Singular words tumbled from her in an incoherent erotic mess. But he didn't do as she begged. He just kept teasing her with that devilish touch until she thrashed beneath him then utterly strung out, she arched one last time.

'Oh, no...' she shuddered.

'You don't like that?' he rasped. 'You don't want—?'

'I want you *inside* me...' she moaned.

But it was too late. She shuddered as waves of bliss tumbled over her until, wrecked, all she could do was gasp for air. He chuckled and slowly nudged the thin straps from her shoulders. Soon she wore only the diamonds. He touched them, then lifted his gaze. She was simply a puddle of goo in the heat of his blue eyes.

She didn't strip him. Yeah, that threat had been completely hollow. She couldn't even move. She was still quivering too much. He stepped back and yanked off his jacket and shirt, shedding shoes, trousers, boxers. He even remembered to use protection when she'd not even thought of it. She was just stunned—only able to watch because Ramon was genetically *blessed*. He was beautiful and so terrifyingly, fantastically *focused*. On her. She couldn't handle the intensity of her rising desire.

And he seemed to know because he helped. He was gentle as he joined her on the bed, pulling her closer. She moaned almost helplessly as he braced above her. He slid his hands beneath her, holding her so he could sink deep in a powerful thrust. She cried out, unable to hold back the delight as he filled her. His beautiful face stiffened as his jaw locked.

'Happy now?' he gritted.

So happy she choked back a sob and closed her eyes to hide her tears. The only thing she could manage was to kiss him. His moan as he pressed deeper into her was guttural. It was so slow. So perfect. Every inch of her skin tingled. Every muscle was like jelly, wrecked from the shuddering tension between bliss and need. The sensation—to her bones—was exquisite. He swept his hand down her arm, pressing his palm to hers, locking their fingers together.

His blue eyes blazed into hers. 'I knew we'd be good but *this*—'

Yeah. Ecstasy competed with overwhelm. All

she wanted was to pull him closer still. Finally she found her strength. She wrapped her legs around him, kissing him long and deep. Something unleashed within her. Something *he* unleashed. Not just pleasure but power, she found purpose in her own body. She was meant to be here—meant to be like this—with him. She welcomed it. Wanted more. Braced closer. Everything melded as they made love.

He closed his eyes and hissed. They were locked together, fighting to get closer still. Best feeling. Ever. Best moment of her life. Ever. She didn't want it to end. Ever. But his draw was too strong, the drive between them inexorable and her next release simply sneaked up. The savage cry was pulled from her soul and she shook in his arms. They tightened—so very tightly. He gripped her and growled as he thrust hard one last time. She clung to him as he shuddered in her arms. She never wanted to let him go. She would hold him like this always.

Ramon didn't want to move. Couldn't, actually. Elodie was draped over him, her legs entangled with his. Soft, warm, utterly asleep. They were nestled together and apparently had been the entire night. So much for all his threats of prowess. There'd been no acrobatics. It had hardly been a sexual marathon. He'd been shattered on a level he didn't recognise by that one encounter then slept like nothing else. She was still knocked out.

He wriggled to glance at his clock, stunned to realise the time. He roused his will—the discipline that saw him rise early. Always. That's how he caught up on issues from the other side of the globe that had come in overnight. He needed to do that now. So he ignored the inner scream to stay and keep cuddling her and steeled himself. Stole out of the bed and went to shower in a bathroom further away so he didn't disturb her. Though she was so asleep he doubted she'd wake.

He turned the water to cold because the desire he'd thought would ebb, had only done the opposite. He was hot as hell and it was everything he didn't want.

His father had been ridden by urges, unable to control impulse or appetite. He'd wanted everything and had no compunction in going for it all. He'd groomed Ramon to be his heir. In everything. Once when Ramon had accompanied him on a business trip, he'd walked in on his father with his 'assistant'. Not an image Ramon ever wanted to recall. Nor was the 'man-to-man' talk his father had then had with him.

'These things are minor. Mean nothing. There's no need to hurt your mother. It's never anyone she knows, never at home. You play away—you understand? As long as you're discreet—'

As if that made it okay somehow.

To the world—indeed to Ramon up until that moment—it seemed his father had *adored* his mother. Ramon suspected his father *believed* that he loved her. But his greed and conceit led him to think he could have more—to have everything and anything and anyone he wanted. And he did. Less than a year later his father had died while in the company of one of his lovers. Ramon had moved mountains to keep that horrible secret safe from his mother and he'd succeeded until her own sister—Cristina—had revealed something far worse.

Ramon was a lot like his father—fully *success* driven. He'd feared it would take nothing to tip into that same world of greed and excess, so he restrained himself. Never made promises he couldn't keep—never allowed a lover to consume his thoughts or influence his choices. He'd never intended to marry and definitely didn't need heirs to dump his driven nature onto. He'd relished his work and would work until the day he died. It had satisfied him completely.

Until he'd met her.

Now Ramon finally understood why and how his father had just 'needed more'. Elodie Wallace had activated his libidinous gene. All he could think about was going back to bed and taking up from where last night had ended. Because it had been amazing. Yet their intimacy had gone differently to how he'd expected. She'd talked a big game but the second he'd actually touched her she'd rapidly become so overwhelmed it was almost as if she'd been *shy*. Her fingers had curled in and she'd only been able to gasp as he'd tasted her. She'd certainly been *sweet*. He'd been happy to take the lead and in doing so it had become evident that she adored sex. Which was good. Being as insatiable as each other meant they could burn this out. For his own peace of mind he needed it to burn out *quickly*.

He looked in on her and mentally willed her to wake. She didn't. She was so deep in slumber that he felt like a stalker. He went back to his office, printed off the document that had arrived in his inbox, spent an hour reading it before realising not one word had sunk in. Then he returned to his bedroom—delighted to see her sharp eyes open. He could only see to her shoulders because she was snuggled beneath the sheet. Her hair was somewhat wild and her face flushed, and she was still wearing the diamond necklace.

'You should send another proof-of-life picture,' he said huskily. 'You look…'

Beautiful. Like an utterly irresistible living jewel.

'What?' She eyed him warily.

'Cute,' he completely understated, reaching for some defence against his weakness. 'Didn't expect you'd be so cuddly.'

She stiffened. 'Apologies if I overstepped.'

'No, you were sweet. I slept well.'

Her expression pinched. 'So glad.'

He laughed. 'And you didn't?' He tossed the papers beside her and thrust his hands back in his pockets. He could practice self-restraint. Sure he could.

'What's this?' she looked sniffy.

'Your wedding present.'

She scanned the first page. 'You've bought the building? Not just the business?' She nudged the offending document with a single finger until it fell from the bed to the floor. 'This is more than we agreed,' she said coldly.

His adrenaline surged. She wanted to reject it. She wasn't just reactive or responsive, but volatile as hell. He liked it—liked that she let him know the second she was unhappy about something. That at moments like this, she held nothing back.

'Spectacular as it was, this isn't a bonus for last night.' He couldn't resist stepping closer. 'Consider it payment for your vow of obedience yesterday.'

'What?' She sat bolt upright, clutching the sheet to her beautiful body. 'I never vowed obedience.'

'Didn't you understand the Spanish?' he inquired innocently. 'I think it had a slightly different meaning.'

'Rubbish.'

'It is so easy to aggravate you.' He laughed again. 'Now you own the building you can really go to town. Put in that flood room and you can drown the most annoying customers.'

'Don't put ideas in my head.'

'You already have ideas. Sadly, there isn't the time to enact them right now. That is why I'm keeping my distance. Your temptress wiles will not work on me this morning.'

Who was he kidding. He was going to act on them.

'Wiles?' She held the sheet to her neck and awkwardly swivelled to get out of bed, dragging the linen with her across the room. 'I'm not doing anything. You're the one with the apparent need to *flex*.'

Yeah, he had no idea why he'd thought he should get dressed earlier. Dumbest idea ever. And if she still wanted him to take the lead, he'd do so. Happily. He trod on the edge of the sheet. She stopped seven paces from the bed. Tugged. He didn't relent—rather, he took two handfuls of the thing and pulled it right off her. Delighted when she was suddenly naked before him.

She glared even as colour tinged her from top to toe. Only then she flicked her hair and turned her back. Possessive fire destroyed his soul.

'Don't turn away from me.' He was on her in two paces and spun her to face him. Embarrassingly, his words were a strangled plea. 'Look at me,' he muttered breathlessly. 'Right at me.'

'Why?'

Because she couldn't hide her response to him when she faced him and he needed that desperately. Because he didn't want her to shut him out. He needed to see the heat and longing she couldn't suppress. For *him*.

'So you can't pretend to yourself that it isn't me who does this to you,' he growled. 'That it's *me* you want more of.'

Yeah, he got off on that in a way he wasn't sure was altogether healthy. More than a desire, it was a desperate need. He growled, pushing out that disturbing thought. He'd reduce her to that writhing beauty again—squirming and sighing at his touch—where the only word she could utter was his name. That was all he needed.

'Egotist.' But she faced him and her body flushed with desire.

He stripped off his tee, observing with keen pleasure the colour flame across her face. 'Yeah, but you can't deny it.'

He shoved down his jeans and she stepped towards him. He went in low, scooped her up and tumbled her back to the bed. This time there were few preliminaries. No matter. He was hard. She was hot and wet. He gazed into her eyes as he thrust home. He liked the excitement she couldn't hide from him. Liked seeing her lose total control the second before he lost his.

It was over far too quickly. But this time he wasn't wiped out. He was energised.

'Not enough,' he muttered.

He filled the bath and took her in there. Propelled her to the kitchen for sustenance and ended up taking her there again too. Then he'd had to carry her back to bed where hours passed in a haze of sexual hunger and fulfilment which was exactly what he needed. They would burn this out.

He woke with a start. Swore as he blinked at the time.

'Wake up, *cariño*.' He shook her shoulders gently. 'Get dressed for the evening. We'll take the helicopter.'

CHAPTER NINE

ELODIE COMBED HER HAIR, trying to convince herself she had herself together—as if this were the sort of thing she did on the daily. Being transported in chauffeured cars and private planes accompanied by bodyguards because she was accompanying a stupendously wealthy man was no problem...and actually all that she *could* handle.

But facing her father for the first time in years? That was the emotional catastrophe causing her nausea right now. Not Ramon. Not the fact that he'd got out of bed early this morning without her even being aware of it. Not that he'd showered and dressed and continued his campaign of corporate domination while she had no idea what time it was or where her panties were. She'd thought she'd finally got herself together after the incredible experience he'd given her last night but then he'd flummoxed her with the gift of the building and then they'd spent most of the day in bed.

Shockingly, it wasn't enough. She'd thought last night would salve her sensual ache, not make it *worse*. But it was definitely worse even *after* to-day's luxurious sensual marathon. And the problem was that if everything went to plan tonight, both their other 'needs' would be met. Ashleigh's engagement would be ended while Ramon would have the paperwork to secure that property. There'd be no reason for their 'marriage' to last that much longer. She was sure he wasn't serious about the six months. From the little she could gather online, the man had short relationships and not many because he was ruthlessly focused on his work.

So actually Ramon totally bothered her. Or rather the feelings he aroused in her did. And now she had to face her *father* as well and she hadn't faced him in years.

She would need every ounce of armour to get through the ordeal. She built it from the ground up—shoes, dress, jewellery, make-up, hair. She knew the purple gown was striking, especially with the diamonds glittering and the fake ruby gleaming. It ought to be too much but for an occasion like this it was perfectly over the top. She stepped out to meet him, eyes widening when she saw his suit. Immaculately tailored, it was the colour of her ruby engagement ring. Again, it should clash with her purple, but they were a match. Sartorially. Sexually.

That hunger in her awakened anew. 'I'm impressed,' she muttered almost grudgingly.

'At last,' he said dryly before flashing her a wicked grin. 'I like dressing up for you, Elodie. I like you dressing up for me. I like *undressing* you even more. But all our efforts will have been for nothing if we don't even make it out the door. '

He made her laugh. If he'd really done it to please her it had worked.

She ran her thumb over the back of her ring. 'You really think your cousin will call off this engagement just because you're married?'

'I'm certain he will.'

Quelling those rising nerves, she stared out of the window of the helicopter and then in the car, not bothered that Ramon worked the entire time. It gave her a chance to practice breathing. She needed to—her lungs grew more constricted the nearer they got.

'How long since you've been back?' He broke into her spiralling thoughts.

She realised the car was approaching her parents' place and went cold all over. 'Over three years.'

The hotel's former seaside glory was long gone. Honestly, she was surprised it was still standing. Her father—for all his loud bluster—wasn't the best businessman, cut corners on upkeep and it was probably only because of the stunning views and the proximity to the sea that it had survived this long. Well, that and the tireless work her mother and sister did behind the scenes.

'You didn't miss it?' He watched her.

'The beach, absolutely.' But not the endless unpaid shifts as housemaid. She felt bad she'd left her sister to do that on her own.

'I moved to London and fell on my feet at that job at the escape room. I was so lucky.'

She'd met Phoebe there on one of her first shifts when Phoebe had been a guest on a corporate team-building day. It had been the start of the best friendship. And she'd grown confidence in discovering she was good at the work. The increasing responsibility and the respect the owner had given her had proven it. But all that confidence fled from her now.

'How are we going to do this?' She had to actively draw in a breath.

'As quickly as possible,' Ramon said. 'So I can have you alone again.' He took her hand and gave it a comforting squeeze.

But as they walked inside she felt as if she were walking into an icebox. Never had she been so cold. He slowed on their way through the reception area and frowned at the frames behind the counter.

'You're excluded from family photos?'

'They trade on it being a family hotel.' Elodie winced. 'My behaviour was not "family-friendly".'

Ramon turned to her. 'But still—'

'We're *possessions* to him, not really people.' She let go of his hand to rub the tension from her forehead. It was hard to explain how it happened, how someone could have control over others in such an overwhelming, undeniable way. 'It

was important we make him look good—that we
didn't disrespect him, that we made him proud.
His word was law—there was no compromise. He
wasn't willing to listen to alternative ideas. Not
from me anyway.'

Ramon rolled his shoulders. 'Your mother
didn't stand up to him? Your ex-husband?'

She dropped her hand and straightened. 'It
doesn't matter—I shouldn't need anyone to stand
up for me. I should be able to handle it myself.'

She moved. There was no point delaying this.
Ramon walked beside her as she moved towards
the private function room. The door was ajar and
she heard a polite laugh. When they walked in
almost everyone in the room turned. She caught
Ashleigh's eye and inwardly winced at her sister's desperate look of relief. But then she saw her
father's expression—shock, swiftly followed by
rage. Yeah, he didn't like surprises. Didn't like not
knowing what was going on—because that made
his control vulnerable.

But suddenly Elodie wasn't the capable, confident person she'd thought she'd become. She was
a girl again. Afraid of displeasing the man who
demanded complete obedience over everything.
In a nanosecond she was entirely paralysed.

Her father stepped forward. 'Who are—?'

'Ramon Fernandez,' Ramon interrupted coolly.
'Elodie's husband.'

Everyone stared—stunned—including Elodie,

because she hadn't expected him to just come out with it like that. But of course Ramon was nothing if not quick once he'd decided upon an action.

'Full marks for dramatic entrance, no?' he murmured as he put a firm hand on her back and guided her forward to claim centre space in the room.

Elodie shot him a brittle smile of appreciation and cowardly as it was, allowed him to take the lead. He wasn't a cat amongst the pigeons, he was a panther. Sleek and predatory and totally at ease, and she was so grateful because he gave her a chance to breathe.

'You're...*what*?' her father asked.

'With two such happy occasions this is the perfect time for us all to reunite, don't you agree?' Ramon picked up a cocktail and raised the glass.

No one agreed. No one said anything. But life began to trickle back into Elodie.

'I wasn't aware of it until recently, but it is amazing to consider our families' double connection.' Ramon sipped before immediately setting the glass down as if the taste had displeased him. 'Of course Elodie and I don't want to overshadow your upcoming celebrations, cousin.' Ramon appeared regretful as he turned to the young man on the other side of her father. 'Perhaps you ought to consider delaying your announcement—'

'*What?*' Elodie's father turned puce.

'Better still,' Ramon continued, unperturbed by the interruption. 'Cancel it completely.'

And that was definitely an order, not a suggestion.

Elodie had thought it would amuse Ramon to do this; instead she sensed he was actually battling a deep anger that went beyond her understanding.

'You're not… You can't…' Her father stepped forward. 'You're—'

'Ramon Fernandez,' Ramon repeated patiently. 'Chair of Fernandez Group Holdings. Your daughter Elodie's husband.'

Ashleigh had covered her mouth with her hand and had been slowly edging closer and closer to Elodie this whole time. 'Elodie?'

'One celebration at a time, I think,' Ramon said as if it were all settled. 'After all, Ashleigh is young. She hasn't had much opportunity to see the world. Don't you agree?'

Again, no one agreed.

Elodie looked at the well-dressed woman standing alongside her mother. It had to be Ramon's aunt. She was younger than Elodie had imagined her to be—formidable and clearly furious. His cousin's face was awash with colour and he fidgeted until his mother said something sharp in Spanish that stilled him.

'Ashleigh.' Ramon turned and addressed her sister in a far gentler tone. 'It would be our pleasure if you would join Elodie and me in London. Take a break from the pressures here. Would you like that?'

Ashleigh's eyes widened.

'Ash—'

'Don't interrupt, Dad.' Elodie finally remembered she had a spine and spoke firmly. 'This is her choice.'

She looked her ruddy-faced father in the eyes and felt a completely foreign calm enter, easing her lungs as she stared him down. And for once he fell silent.

'Is that okay?' Ashleigh breathed right beside her. 'Would that be okay?'

'Of course. Go pack a bag.' Elodie nodded. 'Be quick.'

Her father's eyes narrowed, taking in her dress, her diamonds. 'You're really married?'

'Yes.'

It really seemed to be taking him a while to process it. Elodie glanced just beyond him to where her mother stood a step back. She'd paled but remained silent as always in any kind of 'situation'. Elodie willed her to say *something*, to speak up just for once. But she didn't. Maybe she never would. Maybe she'd been browbeaten too long. That was when Elodie's heart ached.

'I'll take care of her, Mum,' she said softly.

She should have got Ashleigh away sooner.

'What about the engagement party?' Her father spoke before her mother could even open her mouth. 'We have people coming—'

'As I said, cancel it,' Ramon ordered harshly. 'If

you're relying on *either* of your daughters' matrimonial statuses to boost your business, then you might want to revisit your business plan.'

But Elodie's father had no shame. 'It's very kind of you to take Ashleigh on a holiday.' The switch to sycophant was laughably swift. 'Perhaps you and Elodie will soon visit us again and stay. It would be nice to get to know you.'

Nice? Elodie gaped. His volte-face was completely mortifying and yet so predictable. Always he turned to the *man*—especially if he had money.

But Ramon turned to her. 'That's entirely Elodie's decision.'

Elodie met his gaze. It was her time to say something, anything—*all* the things—but in the end there was little to say at all.

'I don't think I'll be back,' she said quietly.

There was a sharp silence.

Elodie wanted to leave, indeed she turned but then that stylish woman who'd been so quiet stepped towards Ramon.

'You can't let him have anything, can you?'

Ramon barely glanced her way. 'She's eighteen, Cristina, what were you thinking?'

'That she's fortunate to make such a good marriage so young.'

Ramon's dismissive stance didn't fool Elodie. She sensed that the anger she'd seen moments before was now rage.

'Neither Ashleigh nor Jose Ramon ought to endure such extreme parental pressure,' Ramon said harshly.

His aunt laughed. It was the bitterest thing Elodie had ever heard.

'As if you're doing this for him?' Cristina scoffed. '*You* got *everything*. Why shouldn't he inherit something? Isn't he *owed* that?'

'You think I got everything?' Ramon shot back. 'I inherited isolation and pressure. I sacrificed everything to prove myself worthy.'

Elodie moved closer and slid her hand into his.

'Are your dividends and allowances not enough?' he added. 'I can make adjustments if you need, but Jose Ramon is *owed* his liberty. Give him space to find a job for himself. A wife for himself. One he wants when he's actually *ready*.'

'Like you have?' his aunt questioned sarcastically.

'Exactly,' he snapped.

'You're every bit as selfish as your father,' she spat. 'A dog in the manger. You don't want it but you don't want anyone else to have it either. You haven't been there in *years*—'

'Actually, Elodie and I are going there for our honeymoon.' Ramon's grip on Elodie's fingers tightened. 'And now we've seen you to offer our congratulations—or should that be *commiserations*—we can leave immediately.'

CHAPTER TEN

ELODIE BIT THE inside of her lip, holding back a million questions. What had Ramon's aunt been on about? Why was there so much animosity between them? Where was it that Ramon was supposedly taking her tomorrow? And *what* honeymoon?

He didn't explain. Didn't actually speak to her. He was too busy talking with Ashleigh for the entire journey back to London. Light, easy conversation—never mentioning her father or his family and the horrible experience they'd all just endured.

Elodie battled to suppress her rising jealousy because she knew if it were just the two of them travelling, Ramon would have his head in work for the duration. Once they got to his Belgravia house she took Ashleigh to a guest room and settled her in. Piotr then proved his worth again by delivering them snacks, so it was well more than an hour before she left her sister and went in search of Ramon. He was in his home office staring out the window into the dimly lit street. Residual emotion emanated from him, compelling Elodie closer.

'Ashleigh has everything she needs?' he asked roughly.

'Yes, thank you.'

'She's very polite,' he muttered. 'Hopefully spending some time with you will cure her of a lifetime of mute compliance. She could do with some of your spirit.' He fidgeted with his cuffs. 'Did it take long for you to recover yours?'

Elodie stopped moving towards him.

'You froze when you saw your father.' He speared her with that intent gaze.

Yeah, she'd gone full 'rabbit in the headlights'. She was close to that again now as embarrassment—and wariness—surged.

'Only for a moment,' he added softly. 'Then you were back.'

She nodded. Because he'd been beside her and he'd stepped in for that second when she couldn't speak. She cleared her throat, wanting to move forward. 'What's this place your aunt meant?'

His mouth compressed. 'A private island off the coast of Spain. Lifelong occupancy rights go to the eldest married male of the family. It's for his personal use. Wider family can only visit upon his invitation.'

'Sounds exclusive and somewhat unfair.'

'Life isn't fair,' he said briefly.

Okay then. 'Your father held the previous occupancy rights?'

'Right.'

'And now, because you're married, you do,' she said. He must have wanted to keep it very much. 'What's on the island?'

'Lizards. Not much else.'

He clearly wanted to talk about the place as little as she wanted to talk about her father, but she hovered, unable to walk away from him.

He sighed heavily. 'As Cristina pointed out, I haven't been there in years. There truly hasn't been the time, but I need to go first thing. You're welcome to join me but it's not mandatory.'

'You told her that we're going there for our honeymoon.'

He winced. 'Yes, but—'

'You need her to believe this marriage is real,' she said. 'Otherwise she might contest those rights.'

He looked to the ceiling. A muscle in his jaw flicked. 'I'd like you to have the *choice*, Elodie. I don't have the stomach to be another man who bullies you into doing something you don't really want.'

Her innards iced.

'You turned *white*,' he added gruffly. 'You—'

'Survived.' She interrupted because she did *not* want to go there with him. She did not want to revisit how weak and vulnerable she'd been for all those years under her father's thumb. She pushed out a tight breath. 'This island has a nice beach, right?'

He shot her a keen look, then *almost* smiled.

Warmth flowed back inside her. 'It's no hardship to visit a nice beach,' she added gently.

'Just for a few days. Five, max. Ashleigh too,' he invited. 'She's only just got here and she needs you. Plus she'll be good company because I'll need to—'

'Work,' Elodie interrupted with a laugh. 'Sure, I'll ask her.'

But Ashleigh looked appalled when Elodie went to her a few minutes later.

'I am *not* coming on your honeymoon!' she whisper-screeched. 'I shouldn't have come here *now*—'

'Of course you should have. I want you here. Please, Ash—'

But Ashleigh point-blank refused, and in the end Elodie phoned Bethan, who immediately offered for Ashleigh to stay with her. As Phoebe—Bethan's flatmate and the third member of the FFS club—was still in Italy, she would love the company. Elodie simply loved her friend.

Naturally Ramon retreated into work mode for the entire trip but his expression grew from remote to thunderous the nearer they got to the island and she didn't think it was because of the report he was supposedly reading. Seeing him so off balance wasn't just surprising, it was actually upsetting. Elodie would talk to him about it, only he clearly didn't want to. And why would he—they were 'married' but it was a *temporary* arrangement. He didn't want compassion from her, nor any other kind of emotion other than sexual attraction. And she didn't want to feel anything else, either. She was strong and independent and alone and that's how she intended to stay. Always.

Yet his spiralling mood mattered to her.

At last they got through the final leg of the journey—a short hop from the mainland by helicopter, then Elodie scurried to keep pace with him up the path to the stunning stone house at the top of the hill.

'I'll set up a workspace,' he said tersely. 'I have things to do before the close of day in the States.'

'Sure.'

She refused to pry and determinedly explored the house instead. She would keep their affair on the superficial, sexual level it was supposed to be.

The home was smaller than she'd expected—more cottage than mansion. The kitchen was stocked with the healthy, high-quality food he enjoyed. She went out the wide glass doors and took in the views of the sea. It was isolated and utterly beautiful.

There were no staff onsite. Not—she suspected—because he wanted to be alone with her, but because he didn't want anyone else here. Despite its undeniable beauty, he didn't want to be here *himself*. She figured his reasons had to be deeply painful. Had he spent time here as a child? With both his parents now dead, were those memories too much? Or had something horrible happened here?

The guy buried himself in work constantly. It was what he was doing now, in fact—total emotional avoidance mode. But in that argument with his aunt he'd said he'd sacrificed everything to prove himself. What had he meant by that?

She turned back to the house, suddenly needing to check on him.

He was in the lounge, sprawled back in a low-slung chair—a glass dangling from his hand, watching her approach with a moody gaze. For whatever reason he was definitely hurting, and an answering emotion rippled within her. He didn't appear to have got much work done in the hour since she'd left him to get on with it. Maybe he needed a different 'escape' than what his work could offer.

'Time for a break?' she said lightly.

'I don't need a break,' he said belligerently. 'What is it you say? A change is as good as a holiday? I visit a different company property and it is refreshing. I am constantly refreshed.'

But this wasn't a company property. This was a personal one.

'Oh, yes,' she said dryly. 'Your mood is so revitalised.'

His annoyance visibly deepened. 'You enjoy

the endless creativity of your escape scenarios. We are very similar, no?' He snaked out a hand as she passed, catching her wrist and tugging her into his lap. 'We both like *this*…'

His glass fell to the floor and he growled as she softened against him.

'But you're all bark and no bite,' he muttered huskily, holding her too tightly for her to slip off his lap. 'Where's the seductress who drives men wild?'

He thought she was some amazing lover—that's what she'd implied, right? But now he was watching her with those very astute eyes and she felt hot and embarrassed because she so *wasn't* and had her faking it failed?

'Most men like to be in charge.' Her coquettish reply fell flat because she mumbled it.

'Men who are in charge all the time sometimes like to relinquish the reins,' he countered. 'Besides, I thought *you* liked to be in charge. Isn't that your everything?'

Elodie didn't know how to answer him without admitting her inexperience. But she couldn't stop herself gazing back into his beautiful blue eyes. He looked so tired. So tortured. Her heart rose and she gently cupped his jaw, soothing her fingers over his rough stubble. He worked too hard.

'Ravish me, Elodie.' He suddenly groaned. 'Make me your slave.'

The anguish in his expression made her realise

this wasn't some test. He was hurting and her own heart ached in response.

'Ramon,' she reproached him gently. He had—she realised—done *everything* she'd asked of him. 'Are you not already?'

'So do what you want with me,' he breathed.

He sat like stone, but he was burning hot and he needed this from her. And she needed to give it. She scooted off his lap and moved to kneel on the floor before him. She hadn't stripped him on their wedding night because she'd been lost to his ministrations but now it was his turn to succumb to the vulnerability of being so intimately exposed. She would strip him entirely—slough off the bitterness until there was nothing but this heat between them. Because it was pure and so good, it couldn't be wrong. And because at the core of him there was hurt and it echoed within her. He was hurt and alone and she knew exactly how much that sucked. So she would take him to a place where his brain no longer functioned. It wasn't just a balm…it was absolute bliss. And she would do this because she wanted it too. She wanted him entirely.

His breathing shuddered as she unbuttoned his shirt and traced her hands over his muscled chest, tracking her finger through the light dusting of hair. She battled with his belt and jeans and in the end pulled him so he moved down from the chair to the floor with her. Then she could strip him completely, drawing it out, savouring his strength, his deeply male beauty. She touched him everywhere in all the ways she'd secretly dreamed of for days. She wanted to find out all his most sensitive spots and torment him. To please him. And as he grew restless, and his breathing quickened, and that one part of him strained... Elodie smiled.

He watched her avidly with heavy-lidded eyes. He liked looking, just as she liked looking at him. So she slowly slipped her own dress off, her underwear too. He wanted to look? Well, she would let him. She prowled on all fours, engaging as the animal he reduced her to. Not degraded in any sense, but fully provocative because she wanted to *play* with him.

'Don't turn your back on me.'

His strangled groan made her cringe. Too late she remembered what he'd said when she'd turned from him before. He'd wanted her to face him, to know it was him—as if she would *ever* be thinking of anyone else?

But when she froze, he suddenly moved. He rose and scooped her into his arms and carried her into another room. But he didn't put her on a bed; instead it was the floor again.

'We can do it how you want, but we'll do it here,' he growled.

She glanced up and saw he'd put her before a floor-to-ceiling mirror. Elodie burned, hardly wanting to look at herself in this moment but in the same second she met his gaze in the mirror. She saw his muscles flex as he knelt behind her. His hands swept from her shoulders down her waist to rest on her hips and her flush spread.

'I want to see your face,' he gritted. 'Every time I'm inside you.'

'Why?' She shouldn't have asked. She was afraid he'd make another comment about making sure she knew who she was with, and she didn't want that hurt right now.

'Because you're so bloody beautiful.'

He cupped her breast and possessively slid his other hand between her legs. His gaze was pinned to hers as he stroked her—watching her every reaction even as he felt it. She saw the triumphant lift of his chin as she began to quake.

'Watch,' he muttered fiercely. 'Watch how beautiful you are.'

But she dropped to all fours and he took her just as she began to scream and that made her scream even more. He ground her name as he ground deeper into her. It was frantic and hard and relentless and so freaking good she just screamed more as he pounded into her again and again and again. He was fierce and she'd never, ever felt as hot or as wild. She'd never wanted anything as much as she wanted him like this—primal and free—and so she pushed back on him, bucking her hips and tossing her head and he grabbed her hips harder. She *adored* it, screaming his name until finally he finished with a raw growl and a powerful thrust that almost made her pass out with pleasure. Indeed, she slid completely to the carpet and he slumped right over the top of her.

Together they gasped for air until suddenly he growled and lifted his weight off her.

'I cannot *believe* your ex let you go,' he muttered harshly.

Elodie chilled and turned her head away from him—hating that Ramon had reminded her of *him* in this moment. Because Callum hadn't *wanted* to let her go. Not because they'd been good in bed together but because he'd turned out to be as controlling as her father. Yes, he'd wanted her—but ultimately as a possession, not a person. She hadn't realised that he'd been interested in her since *school* days. She hadn't realised that he'd built up a fantasy of their future that couldn't ever become real. Hadn't realised that the chemistry that he'd assured her would develop, hadn't. When she'd distanced herself from him intimately, he'd insisted she show affection in public so no one would know that there were problems in private. He'd started to insist on more and more and she didn't want Ramon—or anyone—to know any of that now.

'I've changed,' she said coldly. 'I've got better at it since then.'

'Then why didn't any of your other lovers try

to collar you for good?' Ramon challenged her. 'You're an opiate, Elodie. I can't get enough.'

She glared at him. Apparently he was still angry, and now so was she. Because she couldn't get enough either.

'Have at me then,' she snapped. 'Because I'm not satisfied.'

His eyes flared. 'Really?'

'Yes!'

Ramon was in an even more horrendous mood when he woke. He left Elodie's warmth and stalked to the kitchen to make coffee. He hated being here. Wouldn't have come if it weren't for Cristina's jibes. But she only wanted this island because she wanted to destroy every last thing her sister had loved and she was using her son to do it. As if what she'd done after his father's death wasn't enough? Yet apparently still she sought vengeance for all those years of being in the shadow—wronged, silenced, embittered. He growled in annoyance at the memories that surfaced. He definitely shouldn't have come here. They'd leave as soon as possible.

He sucked in a breath. Elodie wouldn't be thrilled. Elodie who he couldn't get a read on. Elodie who was hot and wild and who he couldn't resist when her face was flushed and her fiery hair a tumbling mess. She was a tornado and he couldn't believe she'd been controlled by her own father, that she'd married young to some guy who hadn't been able to give her what she needed. But she had. Hell, he'd seen her freeze in front of her father. Yet something niggled at him—what she said and how she acted didn't quite add up and it set him even further on edge.

'Out of practice, *cariño*?' He set the coffee down beside her when she finally stirred. 'I thought you had no problem partying all night.'

She didn't answer, merely sipped the coffee and stared back at him.

Yeah, he was being a jerk. He'd been a jerk last night. Then he'd had the most passionate night of his life, and yet here he was, still being a jerk. The sooner they got out of here the better.

'Pack your bag—wheels up in twenty.' He backed away from her.

'We're *leaving*?' She sat her coffee cup down with a clatter. 'Already?'

'I've done all I need to here,' he said roughly.

Cristina would know from the flight records that he'd been here. He could blame the trip's brevity on work. It would have to do.

'By turning up for two minutes—just long enough to prove you were here? Well, good for you,' she said sarcastically. '*I* haven't even been down to the beach.' She scrunched down in the bed. 'What happened to five days? It hasn't even been twenty-four hours.'

He saw her slight wince as she moved and realised she was tender from their encounter last night. Fire licked, distracting and tempting. It had been sensational—the most erotic experience ever, and she'd been right with him, pushing him every bit as he'd pushed her. She pushed him differently now.

'You can't make me get on another plane,' she said mutinously. 'I've flown back and forth across the continent this week too many times already. Your carbon footprint must be *monstrous*.'

'I offset it with carbon credits from several forestry plantations,' he snapped back—adrenaline rippled through him at her challenge.

This was what he needed. Sparring with her stopped the worst memories resurfacing.

Grief. Betrayal. Abandonment.

None of it he wanted to feel ever again. This was why he didn't come here. Why he didn't let anyone close. Yet he found safety in Elodie's sarcasm, heat in the sexual tension that twisted them together.

'Of course you do.' She shot him a look from over the sheet. 'You have answers for everything.'

Not quite. He didn't really have answers for why the last forty-eight hours had been such a roller-coaster of the most fantastic and freaking awful moments ever.

'You keep bringing me to beautiful beaches and not giving me a chance to swim.' She glared at him.

'I'll take you to a better beach sometime.'

She shook her head disbelievingly. 'Promises, promises.'

The bitterness in her answer was more than sarcasm and hit harder than he expected.

'I haven't the time to waste here,' he gritted, battling the bad feeling. 'I've got work to do. Be ready to go in an hour.'

He left her, desperate to pull himself together. He even manned up and stepped outside. A long time ago this place had been a haven. He'd enjoyed summer holidays here with both his parents before he'd realised the betrayal. It was the one place his father never brought any of his lovers. Which eventually made it the one place his mother felt safe. After his father had died and the worst exposed, she'd come here and never left again. Ramon had tried to get her to at least visit other places. Tried to get her to accept help. Never could. He'd stand here and watch her walking down this path towards the dunes and her damned beloved lizards. He'd noticed her thinning frame but she'd denied his concern. Denied him so much. Her time. Her forgiveness. She wouldn't let him help. Wouldn't let him care for her. She'd been furious when he'd brought a doctor—another betrayal.

Ramon lasted less than twenty minutes before turning back to the house. Elodie was dressed, sitting on the deck and eating an ice cream.

'For breakfast?' A chuckle escaped even though he couldn't feel less like laughing. 'Where'd you even find it?'

'Freezer.' She offered it to him.

'I don't eat sweet things.'

'Maybe you ought to.' She blinked oh-so-innocently.

'Not good for me.'

'All or nothing?' Her eyebrows lifted. 'You're afraid of losing control.'

He slung himself down beside her and faced the sea, so he didn't have to look into her eyes.

'I lost control with you last night,' he admitted gruffly.

He saw the little raw spots on her knees and knew they were from the plush carpet. He wanted to kiss them.

'I was too rough.' He coughed.

'No, you weren't. I liked it.' She licked her ice cream. 'I incited it.'

Was that why she looked impishly pleased with herself? She'd not had control of her situation for years. It seemed she liked having a little control with him.

He couldn't resist touching the small wounds. 'I don't like to see you hurt.' Not even a little.

'I hardly think they'll scar.'

'But I bet they sting.' His words had as well. He'd been rude. He regretted it. He frowned at the sea, unsure how to say any of that—unsure why he even wanted to.

'This place poisons you,' she said softly. 'It's beautiful but your mood is ugly every second we're here.'

His whole body felt tight.

'Do you even want this island?'

He rubbed the back of his neck. 'It's an environmentally sound investment.'

'There are plenty of other ways you could greenwash your financial reports,' she said sceptically. 'There's more to it. Why put so much effort into securing this when you clearly *hate* it here?' She reached out and touched his shoulder so he was compelled to meet her concerned gaze. 'Is it just because you don't want your aunt to have it?'

Ramon didn't discuss any of this with anyone. Ever. But Elodie wasn't anyone. She was...

He didn't know what she was. But that night in Cornwall he'd been shocked to see her pallor when she'd first faced her father. He'd instinctively stepped forward and spoken first. After a moment she'd joined him. And when Cristina had snapped at him Elodie had slipped her hand into his. For once he'd not been alone. It might've only been an act, but they'd felt like a *team*. He hadn't had that support before and he couldn't resist reaching for it again.

'My mother moved to this island permanently after my father died,' he admitted.

Elodie's eyes widened, then softened. 'She was grieving?'

'She became a recluse.'

His mother hadn't just been heartbroken, she'd fallen apart. Unable to stand the brutal betrayals of her husband and her sister. And of Ramon.

'This place became her life. She worked to restore the environment to pristine status, made it predator free. It's why there's no development here aside from the cottage,' he muttered. 'It's literally a lizard habitat.'

She'd banned all visitors—made it difficult for even Ramon to visit. She'd raged at him for keeping silent about his father's infidelity. Rejected him from the day of his father's funeral. Told him he was his father's son—not hers. He'd never won her forgiveness and all those betrayals had been a cancer, slowly destroying her until another cancer had come.

Elodie fiddled with the stick from her ice cream. 'So she stayed here the whole time until she—'

'Died. Yeah.' He snatched a little breath. 'Cancer. Sudden and unstoppable. Four years ago.' He didn't want to see the sympathy in Elodie's eyes so he kept talking—distracting himself with other detail. 'She didn't say she had any symptoms. Didn't give me a chance to get her help. It was weeks between diagnosis and death.'

'Ramon, I'm really sorry.'

He shook his head. 'My dad was a glutton.

Food. Alcohol. Work. But especially women. There were lots. Mama was oblivious because he'd carefully have those affairs when travelling for work. Then he'd come back and spoil her. He did all the things a besotted husband should do. Gave her all the *gifts*. All the attention.'

'But you knew?' Elodie asked.

Bitterness enveloped him. 'From about fifteen I began travelling with him. He was preparing me. And when I walked in on him with an "assistant", it was a little hard for him to deny. We had a "chat" after. He said I needed to protect my mother in the same way he did—that she didn't need to know. I thought I'd shielded her from it, but after he died she found out in the cruellest way.'

'After?'

He nodded, but didn't elaborate on those awful details. He'd already shared far more than he'd ever thought he would and that last was too awful to utter aloud. 'That's when she moved here permanently.'

'Leaving you alone to take on the company.'

'I was the heir.'

She looked concerned. 'But it was a lot. Your dad had just died, your mother retreated here, and that company wasn't like some small family business. You were alone with all that pressure as well as—'

'I was fine. The work was good. She didn't want me here anyway,' he snapped.

Really, the company had saved him more than he'd saved it. It was one thing he could control and where his energy could be safely expended. He put in time and focus and the rewards were tangible. Numbers were black and white. He'd become addicted to their constant improvement. He couldn't fix his mother. Couldn't fix his aunt. Or his cousin. The only guarantee he could give all of them was *financial* security. And so he had.

'Ramon—'

'My work guaranteed that she could stay here and hopefully gave her some peace of mind that her family company was safe.' He closed his eyes. 'She could be here and do what she wanted. But she lived a harder life than she had to. She wouldn't let me make any improvements. Wouldn't tell me anything she really needed.'

She'd shut him out so completely that she hadn't even told him she was in physical pain. It had devastated him when he'd finally found out—far too late.

'It must have been awful to have her so isolated, knowing she was hurting from the loss of your father and finding out that horrible truth,' Elodie said quietly.

The empathy in her eyes was too much. He jerked free of her touch and swung back to face the sea.

'I've had workers in periodically to keep the place tidy but haven't been back since. Jose

Ramon has drawn up plans to build a hotel here and turn it into a party island. DJs, endless thumping. I guess Cristina wanted to help him secure it.' He sighed. 'But my mother put the ecosystem here ahead of everything, including her own life, and I can't let it be destroyed.'

'Have you talked to Jose Ramon about that?'

'He's not interested in talking to me. All his life he's been told that I'm the big bad bully who gets everything he wants.'

'Told that by your aunt?' Elodie guessed. 'Why is she so angry with you?'

Ramon couldn't utter that hideous complication aloud. He bowed his head, clenching his fists as bitterness overwhelmed him.

'Come on, let's get out of here.' Elodie suddenly rose to her feet. 'You shouldn't have to stay in a situation that makes you unhappy. You requested the helicopter, right?'

'Yeah.' He stood but he was confused. 'So we'll go—'

'Home.'

Home. With her. Right. His breathing stalled.

'I mean...' Her gaze dropped from his. 'Ashleigh's there.'

Of course. She wanted to see her sister. He frowned, remembering how muted Ashleigh had been, how silent Elodie herself had fallen for those first moments in Cornwall when he'd had the smallest glimpse into her background.

'Ramon?' She reached up and smoothed his frown. 'It will be okay. You're smart, you'll come up with a creative solution to resolve this with your family.'

Yeah, well, he hadn't yet. Not in all these years. 'Your faith in my problem-solving skills is misplaced.'

'You forget I watched you figure out my hardest escape room clues in less than half an hour.' She smiled at him a little sadly. 'But I think this place holds nothing but bad memories for you. I know you want to protect her work, but it hurts you to be here now. So let's go.'

His mouth gummed. He couldn't actually move. He felt like he'd been cracked open and if he moved a muscle, he'd fall apart completely. Because she was right. So right. What was *happening*? She was listening. She was seeing. She was caring. And he was *drowning* in it to the point where he couldn't seem to function at all.

She cupped his face. 'It's not weak. It's not running away. It's not avoidance.'

'No?' he whispered, devastated. 'I've been avoiding this place for *years*. I should have pushed for the terms of the trust to be changed. Look at what's happened because I didn't.'

'Nothing all that bad has happened,' she answered calmly. 'We stopped that stupid engagement. It's okay.' She spoke so softly. 'It hasn't been the right time for you to deal with this place.

Maybe it'll never be easy. Maybe you'll need help with it. That's okay too. But your earlier instinct to leave was right. You don't need to suffer more by staying here.'

She sharply inhaled and suddenly spoke low and fast and fierce. 'What your father did wasn't your fault. *He* betrayed your mother and he put you in an impossible position forcing you to choose loyalties and keep his secrets from her. You just wanted to *protect* her and in the end you couldn't. But that wasn't your fault either. She chose to cut herself off—this place is how she did that. And honestly, she abandoned you too. So no wonder you hate it here,' she whispered harshly. 'You leaving now is self-care.'

The rush of gratitude was so real and so unfamiliar that he couldn't speak.

'Come on.' She took his hand again and tugged. Hard. He just followed.

Ten minutes later they waited at the helipad.

'Self-care, huh?' He mulled. 'That's what you did when you left Cornwall?'

'I guess.'

His gut tightened but he turned to her because he suddenly needed to know. 'Your father was always domineering?' He braced. 'Violent?'

His heart stopped as she paled.

'Not too bad. Not as we got older,' she breathed. 'But he still threatened. Mum was anxious that we please him. She couldn't stand up to him and we didn't either. We had to look good, perform, improve the family position. But never actually think for ourselves.' She shot him a colourless smile. 'He wasn't interested in my ideas, but I actually have quite good ideas.'

'I know you do,' Ramon muttered helplessly. 'He should have listened. *Valued* you for *everything* else. Never hurt you.' Impotent fury swept through him. 'Didn't your husband see it?'

Her expression pinched. 'Callum said marrying him would make it better. That he loved me, he'd help push my ideas, stand up to my father and that we'd—'

She broke off and cleared her throat. Ramon knew there was something more she'd left unsaid and wished she'd trust him enough to say it.

'But he didn't?' Ramon pressed. 'He stayed there even after you left?'

'Until he accepted that the divorce was inevitable,' she whispered.

An unbearable tension built inside. 'He really didn't want to let you go, huh?'

Elodie shook her head. 'But Callum made many promises that he didn't keep long before I left him.' Her glance skittered from his again. 'Lots of people don't deliver on their promises.'

That was true. But Ramon was increasingly bothered by the feeling that his wife Elodie *wasn't* one of them.

CHAPTER ELEVEN

BACK IN LONDON, Elodie was touched by Ramon's kindness towards Ashleigh. He put a chauffeur and car at her disposal, inquired about her favourite food, arranged tours of tertiary options and offered every possible comfort, giving her freedom, security, funding. He was unquestioningly generous. Elodie returned to work, energised by the astonishing reality that she owned not just the business but the whole building.

Bethan pounced on her the second she walked in, wanting to know all. Her friend was an incurable romantic, but Elodie couldn't open up to her about Ramon. Their deal was confidential and besides, he was far more complicated than she'd first thought. His arrogance was partly a protective facade. He'd been hurt—his father's infidelity, his mother's heartbreak and the burdens that had been put on him. No wonder he kept those who remained at a distance when he'd been let down by the people who should have protected him. She understood how that felt. Her father hadn't truly cared for her, while Callum had been full of it. He'd told her he loved her, that he would stand up for her, that he'd be patient. But the Elodie he'd wanted had been a figment of his imagination— one he'd got fixated on. He'd wanted little more than a decorative accompaniment and in the end he'd tried to dictate her life every bit as much as her father had.

She almost wished she could tell Ramon the truth about her break-up with Callum, but he had enough on his plate. She was already testing his generosity by having Ashleigh to stay. And would he even be interested? This was only a temporary agreement—all physical, not emotional. The only sort of affair he ever had and the kind he thought *she* had all the time too. If she told him she actually didn't, then he might wonder why she'd agreed to their fake wedding so easily in the first place. Might worry she wouldn't be able to really handle it—that she was somehow more vulnerable because of her inexperience. He was arrogant enough to think she'd catch feelings for him and she knew he'd run from *that* in a flash.

And the thing was, *she* didn't want things to change at all from how they were now. She relished this—night after night of banter, their verbal jousting, the foreplay before they made intensely physical demands of each other. So she'd keep quiet. She'd make the most of it while it lasted. Because it *was* going to end.

A few nights later Ramon returned home so late Elodie was already in bed, reading. She caught the moodiness in his eyes. 'Something wrong?'

'I have to travel tomorrow.'

'I thought you liked travelling.'

'I also like sleeping with you.'

She felt a shiver of risk but couldn't resist. 'You don't see a solution?'

'I see a very obvious one.' He sat on the edge of the bed beside her with a wry smile. 'The question is whether you're willing to endure more time in an airplane?'

Pleasure washed through her but she didn't want to give away her complete excitement at the prospect of accompanying him. 'How long?'

'We'd be away about ten days. A whirlwind visit of a few of our hotels. I need to check in on them.' He took the book from her and set it on the bedside table. 'You could check out all the escape rooms in the cities, call it a research trip.'

She couldn't answer. Her heart was beating too fast. She wanted to say yes too much, too easily— wanted *time* with him—more than she should when this was only supposed to be *temporary*. Which was exactly why she couldn't deny herself.

'Bethan did a good job of running the place last week.' He stroked a strand of her hair and made that heat lick through her. 'Ashleigh might want to help her out on the front of house—would be something to occupy her while she works out which course she wants to enrol in. She could invite a friend to stay here, an assistant could move in too—she wouldn't need to be lonely. You'll call her lots. She'll be safe.'

'Are you managing my business for me?' she teased breathlessly.

'Your business is my business.' His finger traced down her neck and drew a little circle in that space between her collarbones.

Right now—for now—he wanted her to come with him and she couldn't say no.

Mi casa es su casa.' His finger dipped lower, a direct line down between her breasts.

What's yours is mine. He had all the expressions and used them well. She reminded herself again that this was merely banter, just the light tease that they'd fallen into so easily from the start. But buried in a secret chamber deep in her heart was the burgeoning wish that he actually meant it.

'You should pack your bikini.' His eyes twinkled as he played his trump card and took a side detour to her straining nipple.

Elodie grabbed hold of his marauding hand and tugged him down to the bed with her. 'You mean you're *finally* letting me loose on a beach?'

The next morning—having laughed at Ashleigh's wholehearted reassurance that she was living her best life *ever* and Elodie could definitely please *go*—Elodie was surprised to see an additional twelve or so people board his plane with them. Personal assistants, alternate bodyguards and business analysts, apparently. All of whom were top-level Fernandez employees.

Seated in the private front cabin with Ramon, Elodie was fascinated to watch their interactions with him throughout the flight. They came solo or in small groups for short, sharply efficient meetings. Unfailingly professional, they offered Elodie a polite smile before briefing Ramon on various issues with laser-like focus. Unlike her father, Ramon actively listened, in fact he demanded intelligent input and robust debate before issuing instructions. There was no personal chat before the employees then headed to the rear cabin to work on Ramon's directive. Elodie thought they seemed nice, but none were actually *friendly* with him. Not even the loyal Piotr seemed to have that status.

It struck her as somewhat sad. Ramon was surrounded by all these people who shielded him from everyone else. Yet they were distant from him themselves. Was it just so he could focus on work—as if he was some high-performance professional? Really, she increasingly thought he was a man who had only half a life. Ramon would laugh at her if she suggested it. He thought he had it so very *together*—he loved his work and he had everything he wanted.

But maybe he didn't have all he really *needed*.

Paris, France

'Are you going to spend all my money at the shops?' Ramon knew she wouldn't, he just couldn't resist provoking her.

'Every. Cent.'

'Liar,' he mocked.

'Enjoy your meetings.' She blew him a kiss and sauntered out the door.

Indeed, the only money she spent was entrance fees to various galleries, museums, attractions for her and the bodyguard he'd insisted accompany her. She filled her day happily—returning late in the evening with shining eyes. But *he'd* paced the hotel room, impatient for her return, concentration shot. He hadn't seen half the galleries she mentioned. Didn't like missing out. So the next morning he pushed out a meeting so he could go with her to an escape room, which took far too long given both of them were useless, with only basic school-level French.

Then he took her back to the hotel and endured meetings that went on far too long. He raced back to their suite the second he could. She was working on a puzzle on the sofa. He couldn't resist sinking beside her and sliding his hand into her pants—he'd been dreaming of that all afternoon. Her little moan was magic and he leaned in to steal the kiss he probably should have started with. He slowed down, teased her, making her come before he lifted her to ride him. Her hair was a tangled mess of fire, curtaining them both in an insanely hot world until their orgasms tore through them and they tumbled into a heap of limbs.

'Bed,' he murmured sleepily. 'We have an early flight tomorrow.'

Rome, Italy

'Come on, let's go out for dessert.' Ramon hauled her to her feet when he got back to the suite after another day of long meetings. But he was challenging himself to delay their dive into bed and now, knowing Elodie had a weakness for ice cream, he had the urge to please her in a way outside of the bedroom.

'You're actually going to have something?' she marvelled.

Walking in the warm evening, her joyous appreciation of the architecture made him smile. Then the gelato bar had her drooling, but she frowned when he didn't order one for himself.

'I thought you were going to have something sweet?' She licked her rapidly melting treat.

'I am.' He leaned close and licked her lips. 'Very sweet.'

It was disarmingly easy to flirt with her. Her blushing responses were growing more adorable—indeed her *shyness* seemed to be growing, which was the oddest thing. She didn't always pin him with that fearless gaze. Often times now her glance skittered away as if she couldn't bear to look at him too long. Naturally that only made him tease her more.

Vis, Croatia

'You promised a *beach*.' She looked at him balefully.

'I'm told it's a *beautiful* beach,' he assured her firmly. 'We just have to jump down to get to it.'

'Jump off a *cliff*.' She shuddered. 'Have you not been down there?'

He shook his head. 'One of my army of assistants recommended it.'

She'd teased him about the number of people in the back of the plane that they'd barely seen in the last two days—because he'd been avoiding work on a scale utterly unlike him. But now she knew the extent of his assistants and bodyguards and it seemed she wasn't so much impressed as amused.

With a sigh Elodie swept her hair up into a ponytail and secured it with an elastic. He couldn't resist running his hand down the length of it.

'Not so bad tied up?' She turned her head archly.

'You. Tied up. Yeah, definitely not so bad,' he drawled.

Colour whipped into her cheeks, but his laugh became a cough when she shed her shorts and tee.

'Scarlet bikini?' he gasped.

Scarlet and skimpy and she was going to give him a heart attack.

'People tend to stare at me so I might as well give them something to really look at.'

'Why do you think they stare?'

'I think it's the red hair.' She shook her pony-tail ruefully. 'Loud and out of control. I guess they think *I'm* like that as well.'

'I think you're very in control. Most of the time.' He winked at her. 'I think you give people what they expect. You play up to it.' Her past had hurt her, so she'd toughened up. He didn't blame her in the least. 'What's real and what's the armour, Elodie?' He jerked his head towards the cliffs. 'How brave are you really?'

'You like to challenge me,' she muttered.

'I like seeing you enjoy yourself.' He held out his hand. 'Do it with me.'

She held his hand painfully tightly. He gripped hers as hard back and grinned. Twelve long seconds later they surfaced.

'My bikini slipped.' She giggled as she grabbed her top before it could float away and eyed him accusingly. 'Which is what you wanted!'

Buenos Aires, Argentina

'You really like dancing,' Ramon murmured.

She'd been entranced by the tango display but

now the performance was over and the club's resident DJ had taken to the decks. Revellers were crowding the floor and Ramon ached.

'Yes, I do.' Elodie sipped her drink and nodded. 'No lie. It's liberating. I like being alone in a crowd but knowing we're all feeling the same beat. It's the safest place to express myself. It's sexy.'

She was sexy.

'Go on then,' he dared her huskily.

She disappeared into the crowd but soon enough he spotted her in the middle of the crowd. She had such sensual physicality—in tune with her body, dancing unconditionally, unreservedly, and he could only stare. But eventually she came over, the tease obvious in her eyes.

'You only like to watch?'

Her cheeks were flushed and there was a sheen to her satiny skin and how could he resist?

'You like to challenge me,' he growled, echoing her words from the other day.

She smiled. Remembering. He'd known she would.

'I like seeing you enjoy yourself.' She held out her hand. 'Do it with me.'

Which is how Ramon, who hadn't gone dancing in more than a decade, found himself in the middle of a packed-out club floor. Liberated and laughing. Until he wasn't laughing and he could hear nothing but the music, feel nothing but the beat and the heat—driving him to move closer to her. It was more than two hours later before they made it back to the hotel. To a cool shower. Then long moments more—dancing of a different kind.

'Is this liberating?' he breathed as he buried deep inside her. 'Sexy?'

'*Si,*' she sighed. 'Yes.'

'Look, fluent in my first language already.'

Somewhere over the Atlantic

The less than two-week trip had spilled into three when Ramon extended the trip in South America, purely because she'd never been there before and he'd been enjoying her wide-eyed enthusiasm. But there could be no more prevaricating, he had to fly back to London. Duty called. But he sprawled next to her on the wide sofa, his safety belt loosely fastened in his lap. He ought to be working but simply didn't. It wasn't that he was too tired, he was too *relaxed*. A very different thing.

He idly watched her scribble in the spiral bound notebook that had been new at the beginning of this trip. It was fat now—filled with ideas, pictures, postcards. She was industrious and if that small smile on her face was to be believed, happy. So, he realised with a warmth unlike any other, was he. They were both quiet—no drama between them, no playful banter even. Just *peace*. She sketched and he watched, oddly content when he was effectively being the laziest he'd ever been in his life—letting his mind rest.

But his mind never really rested. Being back in London meant work would ramp up. And other responsibilities were pressing.

'It's the annual Fernandez Family Foundation gala tomorrow night.' He finally admitted the event that was forcing their return. 'It's a good opportunity to introduce you to the rest of them.'

She stopped sketching. 'Surely I'm not sticking around long enough to need introductions to everyone.'

He tensed. Not around long enough? What did she mean by that?

She avoided meeting his gaze. 'I don't think it's appropriate.'

Well, that was ridiculous. 'You're not that much of a provocateur, Elodie,' he said dryly. 'So you've been to a few nightclubs? You've not got any kind of criminal record. How awful for a young person to have had some fun in her life. If they're going to judge you for that then they need to take a long look in the mirror.'

'I thought I was a gold-digger. Only with you for money. I don't have a heart.'

'That's why you offered yourself as a replacement bride for your younger sister,' he drawled. 'The one with a missing heart is me.'

'But if you have no heart, why did you accept my offer?'

'Because I'm greedy.'

'You're *paying*. You're the one losing.'

'It's not money I'm greedy for.'

She sat back. 'You could get sex anytime you want.'

Yeah, but it wasn't sex he was talking about. Not entirely. Not anymore. And even if it was, he didn't want that with anyone else either. He wasn't going without her and he suddenly didn't know what to say. Because *none* of this he was willing to admit when *she* was only using *him* for hot sex. Right?

'I thought I was supposed to be their worst nightmare,' she added in his silence.

Defensiveness—protectiveness of her—rose in an unstoppable wave.

'Because you're not afraid to call out bullshit when you see it,' he snapped. 'Not because you might have partied hard when you finally got your personal freedom. I would've done the same if I'd been stifled by my family my whole life.' He shook his head at the stupidity of her concerns. 'No one's expecting a nun.' He growled. 'And I'm sorry if this comes as a shock but I wasn't a virgin on our wedding night either.'

Her eyes widened and she lost colour.

He gritted his teeth. She'd said she'd cheated on her first husband, and he knew too well the damage infidelity inflicted. Cheaters were selfish. But what he couldn't wrangle his head around was that *Elodie* didn't seem that all selfish now. Seeing Ashleigh so quiet and compliant was sobering because the thought of his fiery Elodie ever being like that appalled him. And while he couldn't stand to imagine the details, had never thought he could ever understand someone cheating, he had to acknowledge that she'd been young. Maybe she'd felt trapped. Maybe he couldn't judge what he didn't know, but his stomach ached and he sucked in a breath and shoved those thoughts away.

'We're *married*,' he said, trying to haul himself back together. 'It's made it to the society pages. Which means it's a little late to keep it a secret.'

'And too soon to reveal the truth?' she asked.

That wave of protectiveness morphed into panic. Did she mean end their marriage? Absolutely too soon. He hadn't done a thing about resolving the future of that island. He'd had no problem organising the contracts for the wedding, for purchasing the escape room, but as yet he'd done nothing about amending that damned trust. He couldn't yet—he justified—Cristina might think his marriage a fraud if he made changes now and he really didn't want to meet with her and Jose Ramon to find another way through. It would be much better to maintain the marriage for the full six months he'd rashly suggested and consolidate his occupancy rights that way.

'Sometimes the truth makes things worse,' he said, avoiding answering Elodie directly.

'So what's your solution?' she asked. 'If the truth is too painful, the secrets too devastating, how do you work around that? Do you live with lies?'

Funny that she asked that when she was the self-confessed liar. But he knew the answer. 'You don't let anyone close enough to hurt you that badly again.'

He saw her immediate withdrawal and tensed.

'Isn't that what you do now?' He defied her wistful expression. 'With your friends and your vows to be free forever? That's a pact to protect yourselves. Staying single keeps things simple.'

'Then why do you want me to show up to this gala as your *wife*?'

Because he wanted her with him! Because he didn't want to face them alone! But realising both those facts made him bristle with rejection. He grasped for another reason. 'It's the trust.'

'The island you can't stand?' she said sceptically.

'I can't let Cristina destroy that as well.'

'As well as what?'

He couldn't stand Elodie's direct gaze, but he couldn't seem to break the hold she had over him. The bitterness had been building inside him for years and as he stared at her the poison spilled suddenly, stupidly easy. 'As well as destroying my mother's life when she told her that Jose Ramon is my father's other son.'

Elodie gaped. *'What?'*

'My father had an affair with my mother's sister.' He folded his arms tightly across his chest. 'Jose Ramon is their child.'

'But your aunt Cristina is quite young—'

'I *know*,' he groaned. Younger even than Elodie had been when she'd entered that unhappy marriage. 'She was eighteen when she had Jose Ramon. She never said who the father was. Never married.' Ramon's guts twisted. 'I *know* she was a victim. I know she'd felt overshadowed by her older sister. My mother was high-achieving and beautiful and I can only think resentment damaged Cristina, because she exposed the truth just after his funeral.'

He shrivelled inwardly, remembering the horror of those moments. His mother had been frantic. Disbelieving. Near hysterical she'd turned to him—begged him to tell her it wasn't true—because his father would *never* have cheated on her. But Ramon had been too shocked to be able to respond. And he couldn't reassure her, he *couldn't* confirm his father's fidelity because he'd known about the *others*. But not that one. *He'd* been so sickened by Cristina's revelation he'd been stunned to silence. And no matter what he said from then on, no matter how many times he tried, his mother never believed that he hadn't known

NATALIE ANDERSON 197

it all, all along. She'd never forgiven him for saying nothing. She'd left for the island later that day and never returned. Ramon had lost both parents that day.

'I never understood why Cristina waited until *then* to say anything,' he said huskily. 'It wasn't to punish my father—he was dead. It could only have been to hurt my mother. Cristina wanted revenge and took it in the cruellest moment.'

Ramon couldn't forgive her for that, even when he knew how complicated the entire mess was. That ultimately it was all his father's fault.

'And now you're paying her back for that by not letting Jose Ramon have this island.'

'Does he really even want it?' Ramon flung back defensively. 'Or does Cristina just want to destroy the last thing that was precious to my mother?' He stared at Elodie, not wanting to see judgement in her eyes. 'Do you blame me for wanting to stop her? You wanted revenge on your family.'

She shook her head. 'I wanted to save my sister.'

He drew breath. Yes. That had fascinated him. Elodie's ready willingness to sacrifice herself to help her sister was so different to his family dynamic. But surely there'd been more to her choice to marry him. 'Not only that. You knew turning up with me on your arm, that your father would be furious to be thwarted at the missed opportunity to form a valuable connection with me.'

'Is that your ego talking again?'

'Be honest. You liked it.'

'I liked it,' she agreed. 'But not because it was revenge.'

'No?'

She looked at him intently. 'What I liked was that for the first time I didn't have to face them *alone*.'

Ramon tensed his arms to stop himself softening. But that was how he'd felt too. 'You don't count Ashleigh?' he asked gruffly.

'I had to protect her. I don't have to protect you, you're strong enough to fight alongside me. You're stronger than all of them.'

He shook his head. He didn't want to accept that she was more noble than he. 'But you didn't want me to bail him out financially. You wanted him to see you thriving in a world of wealth while he lost his precious deal. Is that not revenge, Elodie?'

'You make me sound horrible.'

'You're human. He hurt you. Isn't it natural to want to strike back?'

'Maybe I was wrong not to let you help him. Maybe if he doesn't have to struggle, he won't hurt anyone else.'

'Unless he's greedy,' Ramon said heavily. 'Unless he has a bottomless appetite for accumulating things and not caring about anyone in his way. That was *my* father. That *is* my aunt. And if your father's like either of them then you have a problem because it'll never be enough. He'll never stop.'

'You don't think he'll ever change?'

'Does anyone? People remain fundamentally the same. Their flaws can't be miraculously fixed.'

'People can grow. Learn from their mistakes. Get better.' She straightened proudly, her gaze falling just short of his. 'I'm not the person I was when I married Callum.'

'No?' A terrible regret built inside him. 'You wouldn't let yourself agree to a marriage you don't really want?'

She turned on him fiercely. 'I asked you.'

'But—'

'This is *different*. I get something *I* want out of this.' She threw her shoulders back. 'I have an element of power. Of *choice*.'

He was silent because more than anything he wanted her to keep choosing him, and that was doubly shocking.

'We're all shaped by our experiences, right?' Her voice softened. 'Sometimes we can grow beyond hurt and thrive but maybe some people can't get past the damage and end up stunted. I think revenge only perpetuates the problem. It all becomes a never-ending cycle of pain and payment. An eye for an eye only hurts everyone.'

She was naive, wasn't she? Or—horrible doubt bit—was she right?

'So you would have me turn the other cheek to Cristina?' he swallowed tightly.

'I don't know. Maybe she'll never get over the past. But Jose Ramon is young, maybe all this bitterness doesn't need to infect the next generation.'

'She wouldn't let me anywhere near him.' Arms still crossed, Ramon curled his hands into fists and pressed them more tightly into his sides. 'Said I was too much like my father and she didn't want my influence on him. I was so angry anyway, so busy getting the company on track that I stayed as far away from them both as possible. I just made sure she got the money they were both owed. He doesn't need the island. He should find his own project,' Ramon muttered. 'Shake off the family interference. He's old enough—'

'But he might not be secure enough. Not everyone is as independent as you,' Elodie said.

'You are,' he countered. 'You survived, totally on your own once you ran away.'

'Not totally alone. I have friends who support me.' She frowned. '*You're* the one who's totally alone.'

'I have an army of highly skilled assistants.'

'Do they offer emotional support?' she challenged. 'Or do they help you keep everyone else at a distance?'

'I don't need emotional support.'

'*Everyone* needs emotional support.'

'Okay, fine,' he snapped grumpily. 'Emotionally support me then. Come to this damned gala. I would like you there with me!'

He stared at her, stunned by his own outburst. What was he *doing*? Since when did he ask anyone for touch, for company, for comfort the way he asked her? It had slipped out of him unbidden, yet so easily.

But before he could pull back, she was there—soft and warm, her lips an inch from his—as she promised, 'Of course I will.'

CHAPTER TWELVE

ELODIE HAD FASTENED the diamonds around her neck and checked her appearance. She'd opted for black, not wanting to draw additional attention tonight. She actually wanted to look *appropriate*. When he'd first mentioned the gala she'd been reluctant but she would go there for him. She wished Ashleigh was here so they could catch up but Bethan had taken her to Edinburgh for a long weekend as a surprise treat. Her friend was truly the best.

'Going for the black widow look?' Ramon teased when he walked up behind her. 'My relatives would adore you if you followed through on that.'

She turned. He looked sharp as ever in the dark dinner suit. 'I don't think they'd want me to kill off the man responsible for their gravy train.'

But as they walked out of the house a shiver of trepidation rippled through her.

'Nervous?'

'Why would I be?' She drew on her old confident armour. 'I'm not scared. I like a party.'

'Such bravado, Elodie,' he jeered softly. 'It's the *family* that scares you.'

'Yeah, well, you have to admit they were pretty fearsome in Cornwall.'

'Don't worry, tonight is too public for much drama. They'll all act as if everything is just fine.'

But she looked at him more closely and saw he was paler than normal. Was he nervous too? She wouldn't blame him. Ramon was even more alone than she'd imagined. What he'd told her was shockingly sad but she was deeply touched that he'd trusted her enough to share something so personal and painful. Maybe she could—*should*—be more honest with him too. But she knew Ramon better now—knew he was honourable and protective, and if he found out she wasn't as worldly and as experienced as she'd made out, he'd definitely be bothered about their fake marriage deal. He felt bad about enough already—his father's treatment of his mother, her isolation and emotional abandonment of him, the awful mess of his aunt and his father and his unacknowledged half-brother. She didn't want to add to that. But honestly, she was mostly afraid that he would end their affair immediately, and now it wasn't that she wasn't ready for that *yet*, but that she might *never* be ready to let him go.

She shivered again.

'You sure you're okay?' Ramon wrapped his arms around her and pulled her into a bear hug.

Pure safety, security, support. She knew she could step back at any time and he'd release her, but instead she leaned even closer against him. She didn't want to escape. Didn't want to be alone. Not anymore. She drew on his strength and wistfully hoped that somehow he too drew on something from her.

'I'm good,' she whispered.

He pulled back with a devastatingly tender smile and held the door for her. Her heart somersaulted in her chest and she suddenly knew she *had* to talk to him. Had to be honest. Her heart compelled it for herself. *She* didn't want to hold back anything from him anymore. She would be brave and tell him *everything*. But she would face his family with him first. That was the one thing he really needed from her now.

Ramon couldn't get his head around the fact that he'd been married to Elodie for more than a month because it had truly passed in the blink of an eye. But he knew she couldn't resist ice cream. Her preference for green tea over black. Her enjoyment of detective shows. Her other 'tells' had become more obvious too. He knew when she was thinking about kissing him, when she was about to come, when she was nervous—like when jumping from those rocks. She'd awed him when she pushed through with courage then and it was what she was doing now—looking stunningly dangerous in that black evening gown despite desperately snuggling in to him only moments ago. He ached to draw her back into his arms. She'd given him a comfort he hadn't felt in years and she'd helped him face his past. Maybe he might even resolve that mess properly soon.

But for now he enjoyed watching her gracefully enter the car. She had that aloof, unattainable but sexy air down pat. Her enigmatic focus intrigued him. She liked to set puzzles and throw red herrings everywhere but actually was a puzzle herself. She could be flirtatious, confident, brash yet in the next moment blush awkwardly, flustered and jittery. She could hold men at arm's length. And did. Including him sometimes. In short, she fascinated him and he wanted to know more. *Should* know more. But he'd not had the stomach to ask about her past lovers. It had suited him to think of her as being as bulletproof as him. It had made his own plan palatable.

But no one was bulletproof.

He'd been *lazy* and frankly jealous. He'd chosen not to question the nuances of her first marriage. What had happened? Her father had to have approved it and didn't want her divorce, so had he bullied her into it like he'd just tried with her younger sister? And where was the ex in all this, why hadn't the jerk had Elodie's back?

Ramon had been so blinded by lust he'd not stopped to discover the subtleties. He thought back to those party photos on her social media. Maybe it was all wishful thinking, but he was sure there hadn't been the sparkle in her eyes that there was when she was out with him. She'd posed—performative. Had it all been a front to hide heartbreak?

Now he wanted to know why, to *understand* everything. Why had she embraced such overt hedonism? Had she felt so oppressed she needed to discover herself?

She was loyal to her friends. To her sister. Even to him. Yet she'd apparently cheated on her husband. The Elodie he'd seen, the one he'd touched, the one he *knew*, didn't seem likely to do that. Although she'd admitted that she wasn't the same person she was when she married the first time. So what happened to make her walk out on him?

Ramon had tested her only once with a stupid question about her husband letting her go, but she'd said nothing. Had her silence been another demonstration of her innate loyalty?

So somehow, as they were driven through the heart of London, he voiced his deepest worry out loud. 'Did you fall in love with him?'

She shot him a confused look. 'With who?'

'The man you left your first husband for.'

'I...' Colour scalded her skin, only to ebb as violently quickly, leaving her waxen. 'I don't think now's the right time to talk about that.'

Yeah, rubbish timing. His impulse control had *completely* gone. He bit the inside of his cheek.

Because even if she'd loved the guy, it obviously hadn't worked out and she'd then dated a string of others. Which shouldn't—didn't—matter. The double standard of sexual desire should be left in the last century and maybe he shouldn't be wondering about her past. It was irrelevant to now, right? To his future.

Their future.

Yeah, *there* was the bother. He wanted more with her and somehow the facts she'd presented about her past *needed* scrutiny, because he really had the feeling she was holding back on him. His father had kept so much from his mother for so long and he hated the idea that he might not know Elodie properly—not in the way he *thought* he did. He couldn't bear to be blindsided by anyone.

He gritted his teeth as they entered the gala. The place went fully silent for a second as literally everyone stared. Because she was beside him—his unbelievably beautiful wife. Yet something felt off-kilter. He tensed even more, sensing threat. It was probably just in his head. Honestly, he didn't know who he was anymore—couldn't believe the impulsivity that he couldn't control. Since when did he travel with anyone? Take not just hours, but whole days to his own leisure? Since when did he let anyone in his life for longer than a meeting? When did he hang out with anyone? And since when did he strike her with inappropriately personal questions at the worst possible moment?

Her tension was obvious too and he mentally kicked himself. As if this evening wasn't going to be stressful enough? But there was music playing and a few people were on the dance floor.

'Shall we?' He gestured to the too well-lit space. 'It's safe on the dance floor, right?'

But this wasn't arms-in-the-air free-form fun, this was formal, and she didn't relax.

'I'll be back in a moment.' She pushed away from him after only a few minutes, disappearing in the direction of the rest rooms.

Ramon picked up a drink from a tray and prowled to the edge of the room, unwilling to engage with his wider family yet. He'd wait for her return. While he didn't want to be alone in facing them, he didn't want *her* to be either.

'Why would you want to dance with her when so many other men already have?'

'Pardon?' Ramon turned, unable to believe his ears. He didn't recognise the belligerent-looking man who'd appeared beside him. 'And you are?'

'Callum Henderson. Elodie was my wife first.'

Ramon gaped. What on earth was her ex doing here? How had he got in? He glanced across the room and even from this distance saw Jose Ramon's moody defiance and Cristina's glittering gaze. His guts twisted. This was *too* much.

He hauled his wits together and faced Callum.

'You think that entitles you to pass comment on her now?'

'Take it from someone who knows her well. She's never satisfied.'

Something purely animal ran through Ramon. 'Maybe in your company. Not mine.'

Callum flushed. Good. He was a jerk. Treating Elodie as a possession. A prize. Not a whole person. And maybe Ramon's reply had bought into it but he'd been stunned into snapping back.

Now Callum's gaze turned nasty. 'Yeah, well, she won't give you the heir you want.'

Ramon almost choked. He didn't want an heir. But of course, that side of the family thought he did. Heirs and assets. It was all that mattered to them. Yet suddenly the image of a sweet little girl with fire-engine-red hair popped into his head—disarming him completely. Goosebumps peppered his skin as his wayward imagination fed him another future child—a son. More red hair. Smiles. Playfulness. Elodie would have such fun playing games with them and he would have such fun joining in. And he just wanted to grab her and get the hell out of here because he *really* needed to talk to her.

'But you already know she's probably infertile,' Callum added venomously. 'All that time with women's troubles.'

'What?' Ramon responded before thinking. *'What?'*

Callum's features sharpened as if he'd sensed a chink in Ramon's armour. And yeah, there was a chink. A huge one. Did Elodie have health issues she hadn't told him about?

'You have no right to discuss my personal business, Callum.' Elodie's voice came from behind him.

Ramon turned, immediately shocked by her pallor. Her sapphire eyes were sharp as blades, but she couldn't hide the pain in their depths. Not from him. He chilled, then menace filled him. He was wild with Callum, but even more horrified that *he* might have hurt her somehow and he didn't know.

'What are you doing here?' Elodie asked her ex-husband bluntly.

Ramon whipped his head and watched the way Callum looked at her. He knew then. He just *knew*. Callum couldn't drag his attention away from her. Couldn't hide the wild emotion in his eyes. Ramon knew the feeling. Jealousy burned as he saw how much this man still wanted her. Hell, he probably still thought he loved her. And how had he shown that—by not wanting to let her go? By getting angry because he couldn't control her? If his current behaviour was any indication, when Callum couldn't get what he wanted he got ugly about it.

'I wanted to see for myself,' Callum said roughly. 'I'd heard you finally landed a wealthy one. The husband of your dreams. Are you happy at last?'

Bile burned the back of Ramon's throat. The jerk thought she was a money-hungry predator? *She* wasn't the predator. She'd spent most of her life surrounded by controlling men.

'Yes,' Elodie replied in a brittle, bored tone that sounded nothing like her. 'Ramon's able to satisfy my every need.'

There was the same inflection in her answer that he'd put in his—the stamp of their sexual cohesion. He felt that animal emotion rush on him again but quickly quelled it. Because Elodie put on a show. She masked her hurt. This was vixen Elodie up front and centre and suddenly he wasn't sure what to believe.

She turned and walked away from them both, her head high and her fiery hair gleaming in the light. Ramon swiftly stepped to match her pace. Confused. She'd said nothing to him about her health. Nothing. And he was furious.

She turned the corner, drawing them from the line of sight.

'Is that why you asked me about leaving him earlier?' She whipped round to face him the second they got behind a tall column. 'Because you knew he'd be here?' She tossed her head. 'Why would you—'

'Of course I didn't invite him,' he interrupted. Doubly furious she'd even think it possible. 'I think Jose Ramon brought him. Wanted to create drama.'

Wanted to create chaos. Spoilt and petulant, he'd wanted to wreck Ramon's perceived happiness.

'What?' Elodie gazed up at him and the anger in her eyes bloomed into something he didn't want to see from her. Pity.

'He's *that* angry…?' She shook her head sadly. 'He must be really hurt.'

'You feel sorry for him?' Right now Ramon was feeling sorry for himself.

'I do.' She sighed deeply. 'It must be impossible to be compared to you. And won't Cristina have put him up to it anyway? The poor kid doesn't stand a chance.'

She reached for a glass from a passing waiter and pasted on a smile. Ramon paused, momentarily in awe of her self-control. He just wanted to smash something. What should have been a boring, slightly tense evening had rapidly descended into one of the worst nights of his life. He lasted barely ten minutes more before grabbing her hand and sweeping her from the room. He saw the looks of consternation on the guests' faces as they left but he didn't give a damn about what anyone thought. He wasn't waiting a second longer before demanding the truth from Elodie.

CHAPTER THIRTEEN

ELODIE SAT RIGID in the corner of the car, repelled by her own cowardice. Ramon was terrifyingly silent for the entire journey but she knew there was no escaping the coming reckoning. It was her own fault for lying for so long. Now he knew things she'd hoped she'd never have to admit to anyone *ever*.

As soon as they got home he went to the kitchen and poured a large glass of water.

'You want one?' he asked huskily.

'No thanks.' Her throat was too tight to swallow.

He leaned back against the counter, gripping the glass with white knuckles. 'I'm sorry my family tried to humiliate you. It was cruel. I'll talk to them. They went too far.'

There wasn't just anger in his eyes but worry. She gripped her hands together as shame swamped her.

'Callum shouldn't have been there. Shouldn't have said any of that.' Ramon coughed. 'Are you okay?'

'I'm fine.'

He drained the glass and set it down. 'Is what he said true?'

That Ramon was the 'husband of her dreams'?

'That you have fertility problems,' he whispered.

Right now she was more afraid of telling the truth than she'd ever been of lying, but she had to reassure Ramon. He was wide-eyed and ashen. Too late she remembered that his mother hadn't told him about her cancer symptoms.

'No.' Her mouth gummed. 'Not true.'

'You're not unwell?' he pushed. 'You're really okay.'

'Yes. Healthy,' she mumbled. 'Truly, I'm fine.'

He jerkily shoved his hands in his pockets. 'But you told Callum you—'

'I lied.'

He expelled a huge breath. *'Why?'*

Elodie stared hard at her tightly laced fingers and hated herself. 'Because I didn't want to sleep with him. I told him I had a lot of pain with an irregular, difficult cycle. That was an excuse he could accept.'

Ramon was silent for so long that she had to look up, needing to see how angry he was.

'You should have been able to just say no,' he breathed.

'I was his *wife*.'

'Elodie—'

'I was young, okay? I didn't know how to assert myself then. Callum said he loved me, he promised that he'd help me handle Dad. He had me on some pedestal, said he would be patient and that I'd feel more for him given enough time, and I got swept up in believing him because I *wanted* to. I thought he was my knight, you know? A guy who could cope with my father while also being someone he approved of. I was a childish *fool*.' She flushed. 'And Callum only loved the *idea* of me, not the reality of me because I just disappointed him.'

Ramon muttered something unintelligible but Elodie shook her head—he'd asked and she wouldn't stop now. She'd tell him.

'We didn't sleep together until after the wedding,' she said angrily. 'It wasn't great, and I soon made those excuses because I didn't want to tell him that I didn't...'

'You didn't want to hurt his pride so you lied about your *health*?' Ramon looked shell-shocked.

'I thought it was just how I was,' she mumbled.

'That you didn't enjoy sex?'

Ramon's incredulous expression burned her to cinders.

'I know I'm an awful person,' she said. 'I know it was my fault. I know it was awful to lie.'

'You never should have had to.' Ramon's mouth pinched. 'And was it really a lie? Pain isn't always physical...it can be emotional too.'

Elodie winced. 'I think he genuinely thought we could make it work. He wasn't violent. He just wanted me to be something I wasn't. I could never please him, but he tried—'

'I cannot believe you think you have to defend him.' He breathed in sharply. 'You did what you needed to do to survive. Anyone would.'

She twisted her hands. Did he not think she was terrible for lying?

'So when you met someone you did feel turned on by,' Ramon asked, 'you couldn't resist?'

She froze on the edge of the precipice she'd dreaded. As determined as she'd been earlier, *this* truth made her very vulnerable. She was terrified of his reaction. That it would lead to her *rejection*.

'Elodie?' Ramon's brain creaked, struggling to process the weight of what she'd just told him. Why hadn't he asked? Why had he avoided even thinking about this? Of course her first marriage hadn't been great, otherwise she'd have stayed with the guy. Of course she'd run out on him when she'd met someone she'd actually *wanted*.

'That *is* what happened, isn't it?' he prompted.

She said nothing. She wasn't just reluctant to reply, she was basically paralysed.

He moved towards her, urgency driving him as an outrageous suspicion hit. An impossibility. But now he remembered that time in her escape room when she'd breathlessly questioned what he was doing when he'd dropped to his knees. He'd thought she was acting it up, but maybe she'd really not known. Maybe she'd really not had a man do that before.

Not possible. Just not possible.

'You fell for another man, realised what you'd been missing out on, left Callum for him—no?' Ramon pressed, really wanting that to be right.

She stared at her locked hands again.

'*When* did you meet the other man?' he growled.

Her head turned from him. 'Callum could accept that we weren't intimate in private, but he insisted I show him affection in public. He insisted on more and more—like how I dressed and what I said and stuff. Eventually I told him I wanted out. He resisted that idea. I thought my only choice was to run.' She cleared her throat. 'They tried to make me come home. Dad was furious. Callum went kind of crazy. I got desperate. I figured he'd stop coming after me if I was a complete...' She spread her hands, then knotted her fingers together again. 'If I was with other guys it would put him off.'

Ramon stared at her fixedly. So she'd become a party girl to push away her possessive husband. All those photos of her dancing with all those guys had been a performance. And she still hadn't actually answered him properly. Had there *ever* been a guy she'd actually *wanted*?

'How many men have you slept with?' he asked bluntly.

She went rigid. 'That's irrelevant.'

'I disagree.' It wasn't the number that concerned him, rather her ability to answer. Honestly. 'What's your body count?'

'Define body count.' She glared at him angrily. 'Because right now I'm very close to murdering you.'

The most preposterous notion had taken hold of Ramon only he was suddenly certain it wasn't that far-fetched at all. 'I'm not talking a few kisses on a nightclub floor. I want to know exactly how many men you've taken to bed.'

'Well, you can want all you like, I'm not telling.'

Right. He suddenly felt murderous himself. 'Would it really kill you to be completely honest with me? Just this once?'

'Why does it matter so much?' She whitened. 'Will you even believe me if I even tell you? If I admit to the sanctimonious, perfect Ramon Fernandez himself that I've only slept with my ex-husband and the current one?' She stepped forward. 'That's right,' she spat. '*Two*. You and him.' She dragged in a broken breath and pushed back on him in true Elodie style. 'How many women have you slept with?'

This wasn't about him. He'd never hidden the truth so deliberately. 'So your supposed infidelity, the *reason* for your divorce—?'

'You don't have to go all the way to be unfaithful,' she snapped. 'I *was* unfaithful.'

No. She'd enacted an escape plan. Because her first husband had resisted her leaving and her father had pressured her into returning, she'd acted out. But it had been an act. She hadn't cheated at all.

He gaped at her—so incredibly hurt and he didn't know why. She really *was* into role-play. He just had it all back to front.

'You engineered everything so they'd think poorly of you. So others would judge you. All your wild partying ways and supposed promiscuity, all those photos—a new partner every night, dancing with so *many* different men.' Bitterness filled him. This made sense now. This made total sense. 'I can't believe I didn't realise sooner.'

'How could you have?'

'You *blush*, Elodie. The first time I took you to bed you barely knew what you were doing. No wonder you didn't—' He broke off, registering the humiliation welling in her eyes.

But then she blinked and lifted her chin. 'Didn't…?'

Of course she would fight on.

Ramon didn't finish the thought aloud. He was too bitter. Too bloody *broken*.

Everything he'd believed was in ruins. He'd thought they were alike in what they wanted, in their ability to see this stupid marriage through, that they were mutually experienced enough to handle this affair. But he'd just begun to think that maybe there was *more* between them. Hell, he'd actually tried to understand her past infidelity. But *none* of it was as she'd portrayed. She hadn't even been unfaithful. She hadn't been anything like what she'd said she was.

And maybe all he really was to her was the first guy she'd actually got off with. He sure as hell couldn't be anything more when she'd shared so little of her real self with him. Indeed, she'd only told him the truth tonight because Callum's outburst had caught her out.

It was like when he'd caught his father with that assistant. When Cristina had revealed her affair with his father and the truth about Jose Ramon. When he'd bullied his mother's doctor into breaking his patient confidentiality clause and admitting to him that she had end-stage cancer.

Once more the world he'd thought he'd known was in ruins and it *shredded* him. He couldn't stand that Elodie had held back on him this whole time. She hadn't *chosen* to tell him the truth. Hadn't *trusted* him. Hadn't *cared* enough to open up.

But *he* had. He'd really started to think differently about his future with her. But who knows how long she would've gone on letting him think things that weren't true?

The realisation pressed on his chest. An anchor, drowning him.

'Why are you so bothered about a stupid num-

ber?' Her breathing shortened. 'It shouldn't matter. I thought that you were happy to take me as
I am.'

'But you're *not* as you made yourself out to be.'
How could he believe a word she said now? When
she'd held back from him even in the one place
where he'd thought they were completely intimate.

'You said yourself my past is my past.' Her
voice rose. 'What does it matter if it isn't as colourful as everyone else thinks. It's not their business and nor is it yours and—'

'I don't *care* who you have or haven't slept
with!' he roared. '*That* is not the issue!'

'Then what *is*?' Elodie cried.

This was going so much worse than she'd
feared. But of course Ramon didn't care how
many men she'd slept with. It was irrelevant. He
wasn't jealous or possessive because he didn't really care about *her*. He'd never considered an actual future with her and never would.

'It's the *lie* that matters,' he said shortly.

But he'd just accepted the fact that she'd lied to
Callum. So when was one lie okay and another
not? And she hadn't so much lied as much as not
spoken up. 'Your pride has taken a hit because
you didn't know every last little thing about me?'

He stared at her. He looked dreadful—not just
angry, but deeply bitter. 'Honesty matters to me,
Elodie.'

'Really?' Her emotions slipped and she called

him out. 'You're the one who entered a fake marriage purely to keep control of some property you
don't even want.'

'The honesty required was between *us*.'

But honesty took trust. Which took time. 'You
didn't even tell me about that island at the beginning. Nor would I have expected you to. And
you shouldn't have expected me to tell you everything either. Relationships don't work that way,'
she said.

'Do we actually have a relationship?'

She hesitated, suddenly terrified about how to
answer that. 'We have a *partnership*. We are in
the midst of an affair. We're physically intimate...'
She didn't know how else to define it. 'Trust needs
to be *earned*, right? I don't trust easily. You don't
trust at *all*—'

'How can you say that? I told you things I've
never told *anyone*. And you let me. You listened.
Empathised even. You let me think...' He trailed
off.

She froze, hating his anger. She had to try to
explain why she'd been quiet—why she'd been so
afraid. 'I needed you to think I could handle it.
That I knew what I was getting into. If you knew
what had really happened, you would have had
such power over me. I couldn't let anyone have
that—'

'Because you didn't trust me.'

'I didn't *know* you then.'

'And nothing has happened in the last few weeks to make you change your opinion—maybe believe that maybe you could begin to trust me?'

She breathed, unable to answer. The fact was even though she'd wanted to, she'd been too scared. She'd worried he mightn't react well. She'd been right to worry. Because he wasn't. He was prickly and doubtful and he wasn't going to believe her if she said any of what she truly thought and wanted now.

'And you still don't,' he said softly. 'You're still playing your part. Bulletproof, brave Elodie. So self-sacrificing.'

She wasn't. She was selfish. She'd wanted Ramon. She'd wanted this affair with him. She still did. In fact, she wanted *more*. But he was furious and pushing her away so quickly, so easily—and that told her everything.

'I'm used to betrayal, Elodie. And I knew you played games. But I thought that at least in *bed* you were honest with me.'

She *had* been honest with him there—she hadn't held *anything* back. It had been impossible to. Couldn't he feel that? Defensive, she pushed back hard because this was just hurt pride for him. 'Does it make you feel guilty to know I wasn't as sexually experienced as you thought? Because don't. It was good, Ramon.'

'You don't need to pacify me with half-truths

Elodie. I'm not him. You don't need to protect *my* feelings.'

Because he didn't really care? Right. 'You think I was lying about that just then?'

'It's what you do.' He nodded.

He didn't believe her. Wouldn't ever.

'You pretend to be something you're not and fool everyone around you in some sort of warped protection mode so you can escape any possible threat,' he said.

'While you're perfect?' she flung back at him, so hurt she sought to wound with her words. 'A workaholic who can't stand emotional intimacy. Who basically uses bodyguards and assistants as human shields so no one can possibly get close. You've virtually shut yourself in a panic room because you're afraid of getting close to people and you don't even *want* to escape.'

He turned white. 'At last I know what you really think of me.'

Because of course he believed *that*—the worst thing she could think to throw at him in the fury of her hurt. 'No, you have no idea. *None.*'

Because it was only coming to her now—belatedly and disastrously. Because facing his anger like this was the last thing she ever wanted. Because she couldn't stand to feel as if she were less than in his eyes. To have him lose faith in her. But the three feet between them was an insurmountable gulf. And this had become so much more than a game to her. This had become *everything*. At the worst possible moment she realised how deeply she'd fallen in love with him. Panicked— lost in a maze of her own making—*she* was the one locked in a room from which there was no escape. Not without pain. Not without leaving her heart behind.

Ramon had prised her open so effortlessly, yet how could she tell him that now? He wasn't going to believe her. And more than that, he didn't *want* it.

The last month had meant little to him. He'd probably only taken her with him on that trip be- cause he'd not trusted her to stay home alone, not because he'd really wanted her there with him. She'd been such a fool. It had always and only been a hot affair for him—nothing more.

'Yet you've nothing else to add?' he asked heav- ily. 'Okay, Elodie. You win.'

She stared. Unmoving. Uncomprehending.

'You've secured Ashleigh's freedom but at heart you've always wanted your own. You have it. Im- mediately.'

'Meaning?'

'Go home. It's over.'

CHAPTER FOURTEEN

THERE WERE TIMES in life when a girl really needed her friends and Elodie was fortunate enough to have really good friends. She'd escaped the house the second after Ramon had stormed out of the kitchen. She'd hailed a cab and gone to Phoebe's. Phoebe had bitten back the billion questions Elodie knew she wanted to ask. She'd just led Elodie to Bethan's empty room and tucked her into bed.

The next morning she'd messaged Piotr who'd taken pity on her. Or maybe he was just following orders because he'd packed her and Ashleigh's things and dropped them at the escape room at a time when Elodie could avoid him. She'd moved back to her own tiny apartment in North London and then Ashleigh had returned from her trip with Bethan. She'd sat next to her on the sofa and they'd binge-watched a serial killer series. They were at the penultimate episode when to their mutual astonishment their *mother* had shown up. She'd been wary and tearful and apologetic and told them that she didn't want to lose both daughters, that she'd asked their father to sell the hotel, that she was sorry for never standing up for them...

Ashleigh had been amazed. Elodie had been too shell-shocked to even take it in. But Ashleigh had opted to go stay with her mother at a hotel in the city for a while. The moment they left Phoebe and Bethan had arrived with three tubs of Elodie's favourite brand of ice cream.

'I never even got to ask how Italy was,' Elodie apologised to Phoebe. 'Was it amazing?'

'It was.' Phoebe smiled.

'Yeah?' Elodie nudged her with a grin. Phoebe did still have a post-holiday radiance about her even though it was a few weeks now since she'd got back. 'And the new job's going well?'

'It's full-on.' Phoebe nodded. 'There's a rumour that it's a takeover target.'

'Oh, no—'

'I'll be *fine*.' Phoebe chuckled. 'Don't worry about me, we're here for *you*.'

'Exactly.' Bethan grabbed Elodie's hand. 'Are you okay?'

'I'm really sad,' she admitted huskily. 'I liked him.'

'Have you told *him* that?' Bethan asked gently. Elodie winced.

'If I could go back in time that's the one thing I'd do differently.' Bethan opened the next tub of ice cream. 'I'd tell him.'

Yeah, Bethan had been utterly in love with the

man she'd married and was taking a long time to get over her heartbreak in discovering that he hadn't felt the same.

'I don't think Ramon wants to hear it,' Elodie muttered.

'Then write it,' Phoebe suggested. 'At least then you'll have been honest. That's for yourself as much as for him. How he responds is over to him.'

Two days later an envelope arrived at the escape room with the Fernandez crest in the corner. Elodie ripped it open, her heart pounding, Phoebe's idea of writing a letter echoing in her head.

But it wasn't a letter from Ramon. Only legal documents. The paperwork had been transferred and the escape room business was now in her name. There was no accompanying note. It was nothing to him, apparently. To spend money on a business, on a building, on Ashleigh's independence. To let Elodie leave without so much as an actual goodbye.

She stared at the contracts. She could sell both the business and the building and pay him back immediately, but she wanted to prove herself first—that she could make it even more popular, that she was good at this job. She would regard this as a business loan and Ramon was the investor. She drew up a payment plan, factored in interest. Doubtless he wouldn't care less whether she did or didn't but *she* cared, and sure, it might take her years to pay him back completely, but she was damn well going to. She was already at work on a new themed room and Bethan was busy making stunning props. Maybe she'd eventually expand—she might never make multinational Fernandez-type status—but she could do national. Pushing towards that would keep her busy.

She *needed* to be busy. She needed to have no time to think at *all*. Which was exactly what he did, right?

He hid from everything that hurt by focusing on work. And now he had everything he wanted. Control of all the family assets that mattered to him. Complete emotional independence.

But he did still *feel*. In fact he was as volatile as she—passionate about things that mattered to him. He'd endured the bitterness of his father's infidelity, his mother's withdrawal, his wider family's drama. And he'd blown up the minute he'd found out that she'd kept some truth from him. Because maybe he'd been *hurt* that she had.

That thought gave her a spark of hope—the impetus to at least *try*. She took a fresh sheet of plain paper. Maybe it wouldn't matter what she said or did henceforth. Maybe he would never believe her—never have faith or trust in her. But she needed to tell him how she truly felt.

For years she'd swallowed everything back, obeying her father, not causing problems for her mother. When she'd finally tried to speak up—to end it with Callum—neither he nor her father had

listened. She'd stopped speaking up about anything intimate, deciding never to let anyone in
like that again.

But Ramon wasn't anyone. He deserved more.
He'd given her so much. The courage to do this
would be the most important thing yet.

Ramon avoided coming home for more than a
week. Elodie had escaped the second she had the
chance. He'd gone to cool off and by the time he
got back she'd gone.

He'd told her to, hadn't he. And so she had. Destroyed him.

The next day Piotr had informed him that he'd
taken her gear to her. Ramon had at least known
she was safe. That afternoon he'd boarded a plane
to find Cristina and Jose Ramon. Dealing with
that lifetime's worth of drama was easier than
dealing with the absence of Elodie.

It hadn't been easy—in fact it had been horrible.
Ramon had strived to remain businesslike, stress-
ing that they needed to find a civil way forward.
He'd not mentioned Elodie, yet Jose Ramon had
seemed subdued and for once willing to engage.
Maybe Ramon's early departure from the foundation gala had impacted more than he'd realised.
Ramon had bypassed Cristina and asked Jose
Ramon directly what he really wanted. He'd offered to support him in a management apprentice-
ship role at one of the hotels if he was interested.

Surprisingly, Jose Ramon had agreed. Even more surprisingly, Ramon's offer had seemed enough to placate Cristina. They'd agreed to amend the terms of the trust for the island, which meant no protracted legal battles in its future. Maybe things were never going to be great there, but not great was a lot better than fully vicious.

Trouble was, none of this helped Ramon sleep any better. None of it made him able to fully focus on his work again.

When he got back to London an hour before dawn days later the house was simply hollow. He spotted the small rectangular case in his dressing room when he went to get changed. The diamond collar gleamed on the velvet lining. Her ruby ring and wedding band were nestled in the centre of it. He touched the stone and regretted it immediately. It was cold when it wasn't on her skin. Of course she'd not taken them to sell for the money. She didn't want them—didn't want *him*. He slammed the lid down, wilfully ignoring the fact that he was still wearing the ring she'd struggled to put on him.

He'd get Piotr to get rid of the lot later. Piotr who'd been emanating waves of disapproval like a silent doom machine ever since that horrible night. He stalked to the kitchen to grab some water. Closed his eyes and sagged back against the counter as that horrible conversation replayed in his head.

He'd been *brutal*. He hadn't stopped to think. He'd just reacted. He couldn't control himself around her. Never had been able to. And nor could she. That chemistry *hadn't* been pretence.

For all his supposed intelligence, he'd not seen the truth of her even when the clues were there. In hindsight it was so *obvious*. But Elodie's silence still burned like betrayal. Hadn't she started to trust him? Surely he wasn't just anyone? But maybe it wasn't only that she didn't trust *him*. Maybe she didn't trust her own judgement—or even her own worth. Her own father hadn't valued her. Her ex hadn't stood up for her—hadn't paid attention to her desires. Of course she was cautious of controlling men and she saw Ramon as the ultimate in controlling.

Maybe it hadn't been fair of him to be so impatient with her. Maybe his anger hadn't been rational but reactive. *Emotional*.

Only a month ago he'd have scoffed at the idea that he'd ever be emotional. Or ever need emotional *support*. He was fine. Strong. Calm. Capable.

He so wasn't.

Now he saw that instead of being like his father, he'd withdrawn like his mother—from family, from intimacy, from basically everything but his work. Until Elodie had stormed his house. She'd challenged him. Teased him. Kissed him. Listened to him. She'd absolutely got to him. And he'd pulled her close. Taken her with him. Given her not things, but time. *Himself.* Something he'd never given anyone. He couldn't admit it before but she'd put him at such risk.

He'd wanted to be close to her. That's why it had hurt so much when he'd found out all she'd held back. But she *had* given him a lot already—companionship, compassion, *fun.* He'd revelled in her blossoming physical pleasure, enjoyed her boundless creativity and he ached for her to succeed. God, he wanted to be alongside watching while she did.

And why on earth had he *ever* worried he'd be an unfaithful jerk like his father? Elodie kept him not just wholly occupied, but absolutely captivated. There was nothing and no one else he wanted or would ever want. He wanted to be with her *now*, the only one with her henceforth. Her last, in other words. He wanted her to be his forever. He'd wanted her to love him. Because he loved her. But he hadn't said any of that. Instead, he'd been a coward the first chance he could.

He'd sent her away.

Like an idiot.

But what horrified him most was the realisation he was in danger of being as *unforgiving* as his mother had been with him. He knew how much that *hurt*, how much it had destroyed for them both. He never wanted to do that to Elodie. Or to himself. He was suddenly so very sorry.

Ramon straightened. He did not stand about doing nothing. Ever. He formulated a plan and enacted it immediately. He was so preoccupied that he didn't notice the piece of paper wedged beneath the rug at the front door as he strode out of the house.

Nothing was going to stop him now.

CHAPTER FIFTEEN

'THAT PACKAGE HAS ARRIVED.' Bethan glanced up as Elodie walked in. 'I've put it in the room we've stripped out.'

'Really?' Elodie frowned. 'It's that big?'

'Uh…yeah.' Bethan followed her, oddly fidgety for someone generally serene.

Elodie walked into the room they'd prepped for a new escape scenario. It was completely empty save for one thing.

'Welcome to my escape room.' He spread his hands.

She heard the door close behind her but she was too busy staring at him to have the nous to move. Ramon didn't have the decency to look even slightly unhappy or unkempt; in fact she'd never seen him look as handsome. He was clean-shaven, his hair neatly trimmed, and his suit showcased his tall, muscular frame to bone-melting perfection. She was suddenly, horribly conscious that this morning she'd decided to rot in bed for the day and it was only because Bethan had phoned to tell her about a delivery that she'd bothered to come in. She'd thrown on a ratty pair of jeans, too depressed to make much effort when she planned to be in the back office and not see anyone all day.

'Bethan!' She called for her friend to come back and unlock the door.

But she knew Bethan was still a romantic, despite being devastated by that Greek jerk she'd married, and doubtless thought she was *helping*.

'It's not locked,' Ramon said. 'You can walk out of here any time you like. But I hope you won't. Yet.'

'It's hardly an escape room then, is it,' she said stiffly, glancing anywhere but at him. 'There's at least a narrative. Some clues. A puzzle to solve. There's literally nothing in here.'

'There's me. And you.'

No puzzle. Only pain.

'Apparently this is my building now, and I'd like you to leave.'

'Is this another instance where the opposite is true?' he challenged softly. 'The opposite was true of a lot of what you let me believe.'

She closed her eyes. It was too late for this. 'Ramon… I don't want to hurt any more.'

It hurt to look at him. It hurt to hear him. It hurt to hold everything in.

'You know we need to talk.' He moved a step nearer.

'You could have just phoned.'

'Would you have answered?' His mouth twisted.
'I couldn't take the risk. And hopefully you'll find
it harder to refuse me in person.'

'You arrogant—'

'I find it impossible to think when I'm with
you. Which gives you the upper hand completely,
by the way. And unfortunately I needed time to
think and realise the blindingly obvious. So can
you please be patient—'

'Patient? I wrote to you over a *week* ago and
there's been nothing.' She'd been crying herself
to sleep every night and she was sick of it.

'Wrote me what?' He frowned. 'I never got a
letter. Was it a letter? When? Where did you send
it to?'

Her legs emptied of strength. 'I put it through
your door.'

'I didn't get it. I swear.' He cocked his head and
stared hard at her as if trying to read her mind.
'What did it say?'

'That I'm regarding your purchase of the business as a loan. I'm going to pay you back.' She
locked her knees to stop herself from shaking.

'Oh.' His face fell.

'I don't want your help. Or your charity or anything. It might take me decades but I'm paying
you back.'

'You don't want anything from me at all.' He
turned ashen.

'I want *plenty*. Just not that,' she mumbled. 'There was more in the letter.'

More than she wanted to have to *say*. But she was going to. Just as soon as she got her thundering heart under control so she could hear herself think.

'You know when you appeared at my home that afternoon, all fierce outrage, I seized whatever excuse I could to get close to you,' he said. 'And I ran with it—far further than I intended, further than maybe I should have. But I don't regret it. I can't. I only regret letting you go. I *never* should have let you go.'

She still couldn't hear herself think. Because she couldn't think. She could only stare at him.

'It never occurred to me that you wouldn't stand up to anyone else the way you stand up to me. You've never been afraid to challenge me, Elodie. It's always been like that with us and I never want you to change. But when it came to it the other night, you backed off.'

Because she hadn't always been bold. She hadn't challenged any man the way she'd challenged Ramon. She'd not got close enough to any—all that was a facade. She'd built confidence in fronting the escape room and she'd taken that persona to confront him that day in London. But then *he'd* made her spark even more. There'd been something about only him that night. Animal magnetism had made her *reckless* and she'd reaped the rewards of their chemistry.

She ached for more of that now. But there was so much more to *them* now.

'It took a lot to get out of your father's control,' Ramon said huskily. 'Then Callum's control. It took a lot for you to build an independent life. A good life. You were worried I'd be controlling too. Control is a thing for us both.' He shook his head at her sadly. 'But the only person I'll ever try to control is myself. Never you. But I do want to be with you. Watch you—working, dancing, laughing, doing the things you love—going all in with full dramatic flair.'

'I do want to be with you.'

That was the bit she heard. The bit she needed for that final notch of belief.

'From the second I first saw you, you pushed all my buttons. I wanted to be a worthy adversary,' she admitted softly. 'I thought if I could hold my own against you, I could do anything. Handle anyone. That would mean that I was finally *there*.' She blinked rapidly to stop the tears that were rising. 'You were the most powerful man I'd ever met and I wanted to get the better of you but the thing is, I'm better *because* of you. When you're alongside me, I'm brave. I can even jump off a cliff. You made me believe I could do anything.'

'Except trust me with your truth.' He looked so sad.

'I should have told you everything sooner, but I didn't think you really wanted to know.'

'Part of me didn't.' He spread his hands. 'I wanted to pretend this was something so much smaller than what it is. I didn't want to face the reality of how deeply I'd fallen—how much you meant to me.'

'You deny yourself too much,' she whispered. 'The sweet things. The fun.'

'I certainly tried to deny the truth of how I felt about you.' He took another step towards her. 'You're a sweetheart, Elodie, and I know the choices you made always come from good intentions, but I hadn't shown you—or told you—that I'm here for you. That I'm here for when *you're* ready to talk to me. I know you weren't ready the other night and I reacted badly. I'm so deeply sorry about that.'

She bit her lip. 'You wouldn't have married me if you'd known from the start. I did what I thought I had to do.'

'To protect Ashleigh,' he said.

'Not only that. But to get what *I* wanted,' she whispered. 'I wanted an affair with you and that was the only way you'd let it happen. You wouldn't have even suggested it if you'd known. You'd have thought I wasn't up to it.'

'I don't think I could have resisted, actually. I can't resist you at all.' He reached out and brushed back a strand of her hair. 'You teased me. You were vexing. And you were right. I've been locked away and you shocked a huge part of me back to life. You're loyal, Elodie. Loyal and loving but you should also have fun. So should I.' He smiled at her. '*You're* my sweet thing. You're my fun. You're everything I want—'

'Don't—'

'Be honest with you?' He crowded in and cradled her face in his hands. 'Be really, truly honest with you? Don't you want to believe me?' he whispered. 'I'd get on my knees if I thought that's what you wanted. But I think you want something else. So I'll be at your side, I'll have your six, and I'll go toe to toe when you want me to challenge you head-on.'

It was what she wanted. *Everything* she wanted from him.

'I'm *here* for you, *cariño*.' He leaned close, touching the tip of her nose with his. 'Right here. Because I love you.'

'You're the sun in my universe, Ramon, but I got burned.'

'Then let me kiss it better.' He folded her into his arms and pressed her body to the length of his. 'I've missed you. I need you. I want you back.'

She closed her eyes and let him take her weight completely. His arms tightened even more and it was *heaven*.

'You *thrill* me,' she muttered against his chest. 'I just want you more and more. I fell in lust with you instantly even though you were arrogant and annoying, I just wanted you on a cellular level because you challenged me in every way. You're different to anyone I'd ever met and I'm every bit as greedy as you once thought me,' she said. 'But not for money. Not even lust. Well, not just lust. It's *you*. I couldn't stop myself from going for every moment I could get with you. From getting as close to you as possible. And it was so good I was scared of losing it. So I stayed silent. I'm sorry.' She pushed so she could look up into his eyes even though tears half blinded her. 'I'm really sorry.'

He shook his head and kissed her as he answered. 'You've nothing to be sorry for.'

'Please take me home,' she whispered.

Which is how, only a few minutes after nine in the morning, Elodie abandoned her work for the day. Bethan smiled but said nothing. Piotr actually smiled too as he opened the car door for them, but he also said nothing.

Ramon too was silent as they were driven home, and if anything he looked more anxious than the moment she'd seen him waiting for her in that empty room. She felt his deep breathing and realised he was exercising restraint.

The moment they got inside he crushed her to him again and tremors wracked his strong body. 'I was scared you'd never be here with me again.'

He stepped back only to scoop her into his arms.

'Not the guest suite,' she teased, delighted when an amused smile cracked his strained expression.

'Never.' He set her down and stared at her in wonder. 'I've been a wreck without you.'

'You don't *look* a wreck.' She pressed her hand on his jaw, appreciating the close shave that displayed his angular features.

'I wanted to make an effort for you. But while I might be okay on the outside, I'm a mess in the middle.'

'Could've given me a heads-up so I could have dressed for you.' She gestured at her old jeans. 'I'm just a mess.'

'You're always beautiful.' That wicked smile creased the corners of his eyes and he slipped the shirt over her head. 'However you are.'

'Yeah? I still think I should get out of these old jeans.'

He laughed. 'I've got a three-piece suit to get off. *Cufflinks.*' He shuddered. 'I don't know what I was thinking.'

'I'll help.'

But his clothes were too well made to be torn despite frantic attempts, stifled swearwords, laughter and groans. In the end they were still half dressed when the desperate drive to reconnect overtook them. They tumbled to the bed and the relief of holding him, of being held, overwhelmed her.

'I've missed you so much.' He kissed away her

tears. 'I need you *cariño*. I love you. I want you now and always.'

She could feel his intensity. Knew he meant it. But he wasn't making another move.

'Then touch me,' she whispered as her heart filled. 'Because I feel *everything* with you and it's so good.'

'Yes.'

Eventually they wriggled out of those last items of clothing and cuddled close. It was going to be another delicious day in his bed. Elodie's very favourite kind of day.

'I know you're going to be busy with the escape rooms, but do you think you might travel with me sometimes? I know it's a lot, I'll try to reduce it,' Ramon muttered idly. 'I hate being apart from you.'

'Yes.' She snuggled closer. 'Same.'

'I'm bringing Jose Ramon onboard.'

She propped her chin on his chest to look at his face. 'You are?'

'He says that's what he really wants. Cristina has agreed. I think she might back off him a bit actually. He and I might be able to move forward.'

'That's good.' She smoothed his frown. 'You guys share a father, but you're each your own person. Not carbon copies of him.'

'Yeah, I know I'm not like him now. Never will be.' He ran his hand down her arm. 'We're going to leave the island as a conservation project and for private family use only. *All* the family. I guess we'll use a booking system. Oh.' He suddenly slid out of the bed. 'Forgot something.' He tousled his hair as he padded away from the bed. '*Two* things.'

He returned in only a few minutes holding her envelope. She sat up as he ripped it open and skim-read her neatly typed promise to repay him for the business and the building.

'No.' He tossed that page over his shoulder with a dramatic flourish.

Elodie summoned courage as he paused over the handwritten page she'd included beneath the promissory note. 'You don't need to read that. I'm brave enough to say it to your face.'

'I want to read it. You wrote it for me.' He flashed the page towards her. 'You even drew a code.'

'Yeah, but I don't have to hide the truth in a pile of clues for you to decipher now.' She smiled tremulously. 'I want to be with you. I want to trust you. I love you.'

'I'm so glad.' He lifted his other hand and un-furled his fist.

Her ruby engagement ring glittered in his palm. Her eyes watered. 'It's not artificially grown, is it?'

'No.' He smiled tenderly. 'It's the real thing. *This* is the real thing.'

He'd also retrieved her wedding band, and as

he slid them both back on her finger she saw he still wore his.

'I couldn't take it off,' he said quietly when she touched it. 'There's nothing fake about my feelings for you. Nothing fake about our marriage.'

'So we're not getting divorced?' she breathed.

'Never.' He nudged her shoulder. 'You're stuck with me.'

She pulled him down and pressed her mouth to his with a laughing sob. 'I should think so!'

CHAPTER SIXTEEN

Almost three years later

Don't open the third drawer of the second desk in the first room.

RAMON EYED THE card poking out of their closed bedroom door with amusement. He recognised the handwriting. And he was totally going to open the third drawer of the second desk in the first room.

He'd been away two nights but as Elodie was in the middle of an escape room refit, she'd opted not to travel with him on this trip. He'd missed her and he was beyond glad to be back—even more so now he knew he was in for an evening of amusement with his deliciously creative wife.

He'd jettisoned some of his work so he had more time at home. Ashleigh was halfway through a degree up in Edinburgh. And amazingly his relationship with Jose Ramon had improved. His aunt was wary and that was unlikely to change, but it was at least better.

In the third drawer he found a cupcake with a birthday candle. On the base of which was a sticker: *Games Aplenty.*

The games room, obviously. They'd set one up not long after she'd moved back in permanently—part home office for her, playroom for them both. They pitted their wits against each other with board games, card games, codes, ciphers and the occasional use of handcuffs and blindfold. It was Ramon's second favourite room in the house. Their bedroom being the first, of course.

'I know you're here,' he called out. 'Probably watching me fumble around like a fool because you've set up hidden cameras.

Elodie had used some of her usual tricks to send him on a wild goose chase around his own home to find her. One clue meant the opposite: he was told to 'reflect'—in other words hold the clue to the mirror. The *second* time he went into the games room, she was reclined on the plush chaise longue that was also a new addition. She held a stopwatch—timing him. She must've been hidden behind the curtain the first time. *Minx.* But he didn't mind because she was wearing the pink silk wedding dress and the diamond collar and—if his eagle eyes didn't deceive him—nothing else. No underwear, no shoes. He paused, transfixed by the queen of hearts. He adored her—all this about her.

'Should I get on my knees?' he muttered, sinking to the floor beside her before she could answer.

Her eyebrow arched coyly. 'I love how fast you are.'

He hesitated, eyes narrowing. 'Maybe you're *not* a clue. Too obvious. You're a diversion. Dangerous.'

The look of chagrin mixed with delight on her face confirmed it. He stood up again and scouted the room for something else that he'd missed the first time. Something that was out of place. It wasn't hard to spot. A faux Fabergé-style egg was artfully placed on a low table. Bethan's work, no doubt—delicate and clever. He carefully clicked the lock and it opened. He stared at the wrapped date nestled on the silk cushioning inside. He pulled out the date and set the egg back on the shelf. He unwrapped the date and waggled it at her with a what he hoped was a bemused look.

'You need a clue?' She teased archly. 'Sure. I love you.'

Her voice was a touch breathless. His chest tightened; he would make her more so. Because he knew that while she meant it, she also played with him.

'Red herring,' he teased back.

She giggled and her whisper this time came with a self-conscious shrug. 'I couldn't think much beyond the literal…'

He paused. He was holding a date. Literally.

'So we're celebrating an actual *date*...' He swung back towards her. He slid his hands up her silken legs in a teasing gesture, aching to push the pretty dress out of the way so he could feast on the treasure he adored beneath. But he knew her outfit was another clue. 'It's not our wedding anniversary.' He kissed her knee and remembered the cupcake with its singular birthday candle. 'Not your birthday. Nor mine.'

She smiled. Her eyes were luminous.

'Yet this is a very *important* date...'

Elodie shivered as she watched him work through the silliest, most important clues she'd ever come up with. The man was far more than her match. She loved this—having him return to her. Travelling with him. Living a life so full of laughter and joy, she'd never have imagined it to be possible.

'You're here, another delicacy for me to enjoy.' He cocked his head. 'I think I *am* meant to unwrap you.'

'Well, duh...' She was sitting here in all her finery, basically begging him to ravish her.

His eyes glinted. 'A double cross. You weren't the diversion, you're the goal.'

He opted not to go from the hem, but slipped the slim straps from her. Lowering the silk so her breasts were exposed. She was so sensitive. Bursting with the secret she wanted him to work out.

He cupped her breasts. She shimmied on the soft cushion, wanting her dress to slip further. He got the message. She arched her hips so he could slide the silk down to her ankles. That was when he sat back and studied her—now naked aside from the diamond collar.

'Temporary tattoo.' With his forefinger he slowly traced the Roman numerals she'd stuck on her skin. It tickled and her lower stomach quivered. 'Two numbers,' he said.

She held her breath now.

'Aside from the numbers themselves, I suspect their positioning is significant.' He breathed. 'You think these things through. Your belly.' He looked up, his gaze burning directly into hers. 'Day and month. This is just over seven months in the future.'

'Yes.'

'The egg was a clue on more than one level.' His hand cupped her belly.

'Yes.'

'You're having my baby.' His voice roughened with possessiveness.

Her 'yes' was smothered by his kiss.

Ramon could be fast. Decisive. Powerful. All of which was exactly what she needed him to be in this moment. He had her on the floor beside him, stirred to desperation in seconds. Because the embers always burned hot and it took the lightest of breaths to fan the flames high.

'You're not showing yet, but it won't be long.' He gasped as she battled to undo his damned trousers. 'Oh, Elodie, I'm so excited.'

'Me too.' She was caught between laughing and crying. 'I'm so glad I asked you to marry me—'

'If you consider it *asking*,' he said, and ground into her with a growl of satisfaction. 'More like you demanded. Best moment of my life. I love it when you demand that I do things with you.'

'I have some more demands right now.' She arched, happily pinned by his weight.

'Go on then.' He pressed deep and gazed down at her with the most adoring smile she'd ever seen.

She curled her arm around his neck and huskily gave the orders she needed him to fill. 'Love me hard. Love me always. Never let me go.'

'You mean you haven't got the message *yet*?' he breathed. 'There's no escaping how much I adore you. You're mine.' He punctuated the claim with a deep thrust. 'I'm yours.' His hands laced with hers. 'We're locked together forever, darling.'

'*Yes.*'

* * * * *

Were you swept off your feet by
Their Altar Arrangement?

*Then you'll love the next two instalments in
the Convenient Wives Club trilogy,
coming soon!*

*And don't miss these other stories
by Natalie Anderson!*

The Boss's Stolen Bride
Impossible Heir for the King
Back to Claim His Crown
My One-Night Heir
Billion-Dollar Dating Game

Available now!

Enjoyed your book?

Try the perfect subscription for Romance readers and get more great books like this delivered right to your door.

See why over 10+ million readers have tried Harlequin Reader Service.

Start with a Free Welcome Collection with free books and a gift—valued over $20.

Choose any series in print or ebook.
See website for details and order today:

TryReaderService.com/subscriptions

RSBPA24R